Into the Rough

A story about Golf, Romance and Religious Misconceptions

A Ryeland Press Book

By

Maggie McIntyre

DEDICATION

This book is dedicated to all teachers, everywhere. Without mine, this book would never have been conceived, let alone written.

DISCLAIMER

This work is fiction and is purely the work of the author's imagination. Any similarity to people or organizations in real life is purely coincidental, and no reference to any events, past or present is intended.

ALSO WRITTEN BY MAGGIE MCINTYRE
AND AVAILABLE FROM
RYELAND PRESS:

ISABEL'S HEALING (ISBN 9798650898733)
HEATWAVE (ISBN 9798677313929)
WILDFIRE (ISBN 9798550424988)
A GIRL ON THE PLANE (ISBN 9798573921822)

Published in 2021 by Ryeland Press

First Edition

Cover Design: Karen D. Badger
Formatting: Karen D. Badger

ISBN 979-8-705709-31-1

ACKNOWLEDGMENTS

Thanks and appreciation go to my excellent beta-readers, Suzi, Sue H, Grizelda, Cornelia and Fran whose suggestions vastly improved the novel from the first draft. Karen Badger of Badger Bliss Books has done another superb job in helping me bring this book to publication, by providing some key edits, formatting the manuscript and creating the cover. I couldn't do it without you.

Into the Rough

Table of Contents

Chapter 1

Isabel's Wedding

"You're drunk!"

"I certainly am not!"

Even as she glared back at Isabel in protest, Jane Walkley could feel the floor wobble beneath her feet. Maybe it was these stupid heels she'd finally decided to wear, much against her better judgment. At five foot nine she was tall enough already, without any extra help, and now she was wobbling about as unsteadily as a new-born giraffe.

She leaned back against the buffet table and put down her champagne glass very, very carefully. The important thing was always to pretend to be sober and act the part anyway. But then bubbles rose in her throat, and she burped embarrassingly. She knew she'd swallowed at least four glasses of the bubbly, and it was showing.

Isabel, whose wedding reception she was attending, broke into a triumphant grin and continued her line of attack. She was Jane's oldest friend and took what liberties she liked.

"Oh, yes, you are! Completely sozzled. How many glasses of champagne have you downed already? Not that I begrudge you anything, my love. But we all know you're much more of a beer drinker. Why not come with me back into the main area of the hall, and have some food, to provide some ballast at least?"

Jane didn't feel quite up to moving away from the table though. After all, it was the only thing between her and the floor at the moment. She stubbornly dug in and refused to move. "No, I think I will stay right here."

Isabel, who looked ridiculously so much younger than she did at forty-two, pulled across a chair and gently pushed Jane sideways into it. "...If Mohamed won't go to the mountain...the mountain will go to Mohamed." And she perched onto another chair beside her.

Jane began to lose what vestiges of self-control she had managed to maintain throughout the ceremony and during the photographs and reception line-up. She felt a sudden prickle of tears begin to start behind her eyes and suddenly wanted to howl like a baby. How appallingly inappropriate!

Here she was at her best friend's wedding, the big gay wedding of the year. It was supposed to be a happy event. So what was she doing, sitting alone in a corner and wanting to weep? And in public too? Could things get any worse or any more embarrassing?

Jane had known Isabel for more than thirty years, since they had entered the same girls' high school together aged eleven. She could tell that Isabel knew she wasn't her normal happy confident self. Jane tried to control her tears and breathe out the feeling of panic. Failing at this attempt, she decided she had to alter her plea and confess.

"Sorry. I maybe have had a little too much champagne. It's just I don't know any of your London friends, and I don't have much in common with your brother and sister-in-law either. There didn't seem to be anything else to do except have a drink, or three."

Isabel rolled her eyes.

"Jane, this isn't like you. You're usually the life and soul of the party. I'd love you to meet our other guests and get to know them. We have plenty of lesbian couples here, who'd be honoured to call you their friend. And Bryony, my Bryony, I want you two to get to know each other much better. So come over and sit with us while we listen to the speeches. I thought you might make one. Don't you remember? You did joke when we first told you of our wedding plans that you'd give me away!"

Jane looked at Isabel and did remember. She also recalled how she'd shouted insults at Isabel for even daring to have an affair with Bryony Morris, who was easily seventeen years younger than either of them and had seemed a naïve and earnest medical student when they'd first met back in July.

She also knew how mean and what a bully she'd been to

Isabel when she'd persuaded her to part from Bryony and move to Bristol to stay with her for a few weeks in September. She also remembered what a total waste of time that had been.

For the first time in her life, Jane had been proved comprehensively wrong about matters of the heart as they concerned her friend. Isabel had headed straight back to Bryony within a month. Now here they were, barely twelve weeks later in December, getting hitched in some sort of idyllic haze of marital bliss.

Isabel, who was supposed to be working the room and talking to some of the other fifty or so of her guests, skewered Jane with an unequivocally direct look and said, "Darling, tell me why you are so upset. I can't go off on my honeymoon leaving you like this. Come on, you're my best and oldest friend. What's up?"

Jane decided to be honest. What was the point of being anything other? It was never her style anyway.

"Honestly? I'm not sure what's bugging me. Except that I've never felt so lonely and isolated in my life. All of this...your obvious happiness, and the wedding...it just highlights how dry and empty my own life is." She waved her arm vaguely around the room.

"You know I don't begrudge you and Bryony finding each other, and I hate myself for saying this…but it's just that I no longer have you as my even more wretched, miserable friend. Previously, when I thought my life was shit, I could always think of you and feel sorry for you, to know your recent few years have been so much worse than mine. And now…now you are deliriously happy! And I can't cope with it!"

Jane Walkley, head of Girls' PE at Reedbridge High School, handsome and strong, out and proud, turned her head towards a window and found herself start sobbing like a toddler, one who had just seen their favourite toy deliberately smashed to pieces.

As her chest rose and fell against her blue shantung silk top, she felt very ashamed of herself. How could she begrudge Isabel her hard-won happiness? But this feeling of desolation had emerged from a very deep place. Maybe the champagne was to blame. Something must have uncorked the bottle of feelings Jane hadn't even known she was experiencing. She certainly hadn't acknowledged them to herself before.

Jane glanced at her dear friend. Isabel, bless her soul, didn't brush aside what she'd revealed, nor dismiss it with a quick response. A lesser person might have taken it personally. Jane felt instinctively that Isabel knew this wasn't an attack on her...that she was just reacting to this pretty depressing turn of events.

Jane could sense Isabel gazing at her for several long seconds, and then she felt a paper napkin pressed into her hand.

"Here you go, love. There's nothing wrong with a good cry. This might help mop up those tears if you want to. Good job you're not one to bother with mascara."

Jane managed to stifle the last of her tears, took the napkin, dried her blue eyes as best she could and wiped her nose. She just hoped that the other guests hadn't noticed her mini-breakdown. She couldn't remember ever crying like this in public before.

Isabel bumped shoulders with her friend. "I do understand, in part. Other people's weddings were hell for me when I first lost Carrie. And when our friends have big changes in their lives it can be a jolt. But you and I, we are BFFs, aren't we? You know I will always be there for you, that you can always be honest with me. Heck, do you remember when we thought we were the only gay thirteen-year-olds in the world? How we had to work so much out for ourselves, and what it meant and how to live with it?"

Jane ran her hands through her short crop of blonde hair and nodded. "Yes. But you were so quick and clever. I always felt I was the brawn and you were the brains."

"But you were my hero and my protector. You never let anyone give us grief. You were an absolute amazon."

Jane managed a half-smile at the compliment. "Yeah, maybe. Aren't you thankful that we never fancied each other though? It's meant we've been able to stay friends for so many years, and through so much. You've just been brave enough to take far more risks than I have, that's all. And then, when I did throw caution to the wind..."

Isabel hugged her in solidarity, and said with some degree of drama, "I know, the ill-fated affair of Felicity Fellows!"

"Don't make me laugh. You make it sound like a murder mystery. She nearly was the death of me. And I suppose I've been just too chicken to have a real go with any woman since."

Jane could at least bear to think about Felicity now without physically wanting to throw up. But the scar tissue over that year of agony and ecstasy was still painfully thin, even seven years later.

Isabel was quick to reassure her.

"Felicity was a cow. And a coward. You behaved beautifully throughout. You have nothing to feel guilty about. It's been seven years, Jane. You've done your time. Maybe now it's time to look for the real love of your life, hey? You never know, whoever it is, she has to be out there somewhere in the world, waiting just for you. Have you ever thought of going on-line, perhaps join a dating website? I think you should!"

Isabel passed her a fresh napkin off the table. "Here, take this. That one's a wet mess."

Jane felt a rush of genuine physical fear as she absorbed her friend's suggestion. This was ridiculous. Here she was, forty-two, a dried-up celibate lesbian, who had buried anything sexual deep down inside her for so long she didn't even feel part of her own body anymore. Yet the idea of looking for a new love made her adrenalin spike upwards, as though she was in danger of an imminent attack from a snarling wolf. Fight or flight responses simultaneously coursed through her body.

But then, in a weird way, the hellish, profound, horrible sense of alienation, isolation, and depression she had felt throughout the wedding so far, and in the days running up to it, began to lift slightly. It no longer cut her off from the rest of the world.

She shook her head firmly, and scoffed, "You've got to be kidding! No way, Jose'!"

"I'm not kidding at all," Isabel said.

Jane glanced sideways at her friend and used the second napkin to finish drying her eyes. She realised the idea might be worth considering. Being frightened out of one's skin might be preferable to wanting to crawl into a cave like a snake and hibernate. Hell, to be honest, any feeling would be an improvement on this numb misery enveloping her.

Isabel stood up and gave Jane's sleeve a little tug. "Come on then. I've been remiss and neglected you all day and I'm sorry. Let me introduce you to my friends, especially the gang from "Righteous Anger". Most of them are as camp as Christmas. They'll all love you, and they'll also be astonished to find I know someone as sensible as you."

Jane shouldered her 'best' leather bag and smoothed down her jacket. She felt like a fraud, dressed up like a dog's dinner, but Isabel had already told her she looked great, and the ice-blue of her trouser suit had brought out the same colour in her eyes. "Lead on, Macduff," she muttered and allowed Isabel to help her stand.

Her eyes were still sore and tight from crying, but she knew she was over the worst, and trusted she wouldn't break down again.

Jane followed her friend back into the main part of the reception room, and decided to give it her best shot. She just had to be careful where she put her feet, because she still felt more than a little inebriated, and she didn't want to fall flat on her face in front of fifty people!

Righteous Anger was the self-confessed radical women's aid agency that Isabel had headed for years. As she might have expected, considering it was only six days after the General Election, from halfway across the room Jane could hear some members of Isabel's staff team venting off their frustration, and drowning their sorrows about the outcome.

There was a group of about six folks sitting at one of the round tables in front of a pile of empty plates and half-finished glasses. Three men and three women, obviously old friends, were agreeing about what a disaster the new government would be, even though the cabinet had barely been announced.

"I bet they'll cut the overseas aid budget as soon as they can."

"They wouldn't dare. It was in their manifesto…"

Jane generally stayed well clear of politics, and still retained the conservative inclinations of her parents. After all, it was David Cameron, wasn't it, who had legalised gay marriage? The Tories surely hadn't been all bad.

She didn't often dare let out such affiliations in front of Isabel though, who was someone the Australians might dub a 'watermelon', "Green outside, but deep red all the way through!" It was an insult Isabel was perfectly happy to own, even delight in.

But Jane felt a long way out of her comfort zone and hoped no-one would expect her to offer an opinion about current affairs. She had always considered her radical activist buddy, Isabel, did enough of that for them both.

Isabel had motioned to the R.A. gang to make room for Jane in their circle, and obediently they all shuttled sideways to make room for another person.

"This is Jane, who knows more about me than the rest of you put together, so I'm trusting you to treat her with respect! I'm just going over to chase up Bryony, as we have to cut the cake in a little while. But ask Jane about the incident on the Isle of Man ferry in 1995 if you want to hear a funny story."

The woman to Jane's right, a good-looking, Asian women in her fifties, picked up the cue, and said, "Hi, Jane, lovely to meet you. I'm Caroline, and this is my partner Charlie. These others are Trixie and her husband Frankie, and Rupert and Festus, our colleagues. So spill the beans then. What was our boss like when she was young, and what happened on the Isle of Man ferry in 1995?"

Jane swallowed hard, but they had given her a very easy way into their conversation, and everyone at the table looked friendly, and no longer quite so metropolitan and formidable as she had at first imagined.

"Well, it was when we were seventeen, and we were supposed to be on a geography field-trip…" And she began to recount the story from her school days, which made her audience all laugh out loud.

Four hours later, on the train to mid-Wales, where they were heading to enjoy their honeymoon, Isabel paused from the pleasant activity of gazing at Bryony's beautiful smile, and said,

"You know, I'm seriously worried about my friend Jane. She was so miserable at the wedding. She needs to do what I've done, and find herself a soul-mate, someone to love and to build a life with."

Her young wife, Bryony, cuddled against her and took her hand from under cover of the long winter scarf she had wrapped around both their necks. "Oh, and how are you going to engineer that, I wonder?" she laughed and squeezed Isabel's fingers, and traced circles on the palm of her hand.

"I'm not sure," murmured Isabel. "I'm sure I can find a way if I try hard enough."

"If I know anything about you at all," responded Bryony. "I'm sure you can. You can do anything." And then, despite the other people sitting around them in the carriage, she pulled her new wife towards her and kissed her firmly on the lips.

"Absolutely anything. Even without any trying."

Several fellow passengers looked very shocked. But Bryony didn't care, and Isabel didn't even notice.

Chapter 2

Office Gossip

"What did you make of Isabel's friend, Jane?" asked Trixie Nabieu of her colleague Caroline Patel, as they had a delicious gossipy review of the wedding the next morning in North London. They were both in the Righteous Anger office and enjoying a hot drink and a natter before starting work.

"I liked her. I can see why they've been friends since childhood. They complement each other. And when we managed to get Jane to relax and open up slightly, she was really very funny, wasn't she? She's got a sharp sense of humour."

Caroline, whose first name was an English addition to her much longer Guajarati passport identity, stirred her mug of tea as she spoke. She still preferred it sweet with warm milk, the way her grandmother had served it to her as a child in Uganda, nearly half a century earlier. It was a little indulgence in carbs for someone as still as slim and elegant as she was when she had once graced British TV screens twenty years earlier.

Now, no longer a newscaster, Caroline had abandoned the glitzy world of broadcasting for a much less glamorous existence as head of fundraising and communications for this ramshackle little NGO. Well, she was titled 'head' on paper perhaps, but her department simply consisted of her and their new intern Gerry, (nicknamed Rupert, after his liking for duffle-coats, yellow trousers and red jumpers) and some very willing and committed volunteers.

But Caroline was happy. She admired Isabel and her passion for the world and for righting injustices, however unfashionable or unpopular the cause might be. She also enjoyed using her own skills in networking and her many contacts in the media, to bring in enough resources to keep their show on the road. It was largely down to her ability to spin gold out of straw that Righteous Anger had as much core-funding as it did.

But the task certainly wasn't easy, and Caroline's own paltry salary wouldn't have kept her in shoes and lipstick if it hadn't been more than quadrupled by her long-term partner Charlotte Bernstein, or Charlie B, as everyone called her. Charlie was a professional stand-up comedienne and made mega bucks.

"Jane is obviously one of your sisterhood," said Trixie, bringing Caroline back with a jolt into the present moment. "Even Frankie could see that."

Caroline laughed. "Your husband is a treasure. I wonder how he puts up with us all."

"Yeah, I had to keep hold of his hand yesterday at the reception while he looked around desperately to find any other straight men!"

"Well, there were quite a few there, including Festus," grinned Caroline. "But I saw Frankie's anxious face when he went towards the bar to get you another Coke, like he was obviously loath to leave you alone with all us crazy lesbians."

Trixie sat down at her desk and started to sift through a pile of files. "Francis is fine. He knows he can trust me. I would walk across the Sahara for that man any day. But you know, back to Jane, there was something very sad in her eyes, very lonely. Almost as though the wedding got to her in a way she hadn't expected, and it stirred up some old hurts."

Trixie originally hailed from Sierra Leone. She was the agency manager for their women's health programmes, particularly their campaign against female genital mutilation, or as it was known globally, FGM, where they resourced and partnered women's groups around the world. A trained sexual abuse and trauma counsellor, she often had a sixth sense when it came to assessing people's back stories, and was probably the most intuitive and sensitive member of the staff.

She might have said more about Jane, but the conversation was interrupted by the sound of the old lift doors squeaking open and two sets of footsteps padding along the corridor towards their office. Festus, the financial officer, and Gerry-Rupert the intern, were arriving to join them at work, so the women tacitly agreed to end their conversation.

The following day was the last Friday before Christmas and there were office parties taking place on every floor of their rickety building, which was crammed with a dozen or more small development agencies and charities.

It was also marked by the return to work of the lovely Steph Hunter, Isabel's younger protégée and their senior project officer. Steph was Righteous Anger's answer to Lara Croft, and Caroline was tempted to hire her out to *Rohan* or one of the other adventure clothing companies as a house model. Steph was beautiful, talented, and generally oblivious as to how much of a head-turner she was. She could also be as crazy as a box of frogs and was barely house-trained.

Steph lived in sports gear and out of a rucksack, and none of her co-workers knew how her girlfriend Alana coped with her long absences in remote jungles or dangerous hotspots. This time she had just shimmered in after two flights from Kinshasa, arriving a day too late to be at Isabel's wedding, and in the brief time available, her colleagues filled her in with all the details of the event.

Then, at the end of the day, the office finally closed for Christmas, and peace reigned over it for a blessed two-week period through the winter solstice. The chaos of the world it sought to relieve would just have to wait awhile.

Into the Rough

Chapter 3

Home Alone

Isabel's wedding had been on December 18th, just one day after Reedbridge High School closed for the Christmas holidays. Jane, who caught the train from Bristol for the day, eventually returned home by the same means.

"Do you want to come out with us somewhere after the Reception? Are you staying in London for the night?" Caroline and Charlie had invited her, as they all stood waiting for Isabel and Bryony to take their leave from the reception venue.

"Sorry, no. I've got a day return on the train. So maybe next time…"

Jane knew many other guests had booked into various hotels for the night, but she hadn't expected to have any companions to go out carousing with until the small hours, so she'd planned to return home directly after the festivities. Besides, she always preferred sleeping in her own bed. So, after they had all said farewell to the happy couple, she took a taxi which carried her back to Paddington Station by seven pm, found a seat on the train to Cardiff and arrived into Bristol Temple Meads station just after nine.

Her beloved old Rav4 was still safely lodged in the station car-park and she settled into the driver's seat with a huge sense of relief. It had been a very strange day indeed, one which had somehow beaten up her emotions, and she would need a few days to recover.

Jane had certainly sobered up since lunchtime, which was good because she wouldn't have dared drive otherwise. Her inbuilt morality police were always on patrol. But she'd finally consumed some proper food at the reception, taken tea and shortbread biscuits on the train, along with a large bottle of Evian water, and her head was now clear. She'd escaped rather lightly after all that bad behaviour with the champagne.

The roads to her modest home across Bristol were very busy, even at the end of the evening, so she had to concentrate, but she made the three-mile trip without incident. She pulled into her driveway, clicked the remote to open her garage, and then let herself in to the tight confines of her townhouse. She felt like a dog returning to its kennel. It was a narrow space maybe, but it felt safe and secure.

The house was exactly as she had left it at an ungodly hour that morning. Why shouldn't it be? No one ever came into her home uninvited and she kept no pets to disturb the sense of order.

Jane pulled off her coat and shoes, switched on the electric fire and flopped down on her sofa to watch twenty minutes or so of the late news. She was still full from the very tasty food served at the Reception, even though vegetarian dishes wouldn't have been her first choice. She was a steak and chips kind of girl.

As she watched the television, Jane tried to analyse a little deeper why she had been so upset at Isabel's wedding. It was as if she'd almost become another person, metamorphosing from the brisk, cheerful, competitive woman who greeted her in the bathroom mirror every morning.

Who was that whining cry-baby who emerged in London, full of self-pity, who almost blamed her best friend simply for being happy? She tried to identify her as someone she recognised and failed to even come up with a name. Jane's alter ego was precisely the sort of person she normally despised. She hated cry-babies.

But the depression, the sense of estrangement, (which if she was honest, she had known had been building for months) was like some weird disease growing inside her which she had never endured before. It was a new phenomenon.

Just then, her mother phoned. She knew it was her, from the ringtone somehow, even before she saw the identity of the caller on the phone.

"Hi, Mum."

"I just thought I'd ring, darling, to make sure you got home safely."

"Yes, of course I did. No worries."

"Well, anything can happen in London. You know I always worry about you."

"There's really no need. I am a grown woman."

"So, how was the wedding? Did you meet anyone nice there?"

Jane was sorely tempted to say "Oh, MOTH-er!" like an exasperated teenager, but she managed to keep her cool. "Yes, I met a nice bunch of people; Isabel's colleagues from her charity. They were very friendly, and the wedding ceremony was beautiful."

"What did you wear?"

"The blue silk pants suit."

"Not the same one you wore five years ago to Peter's wedding? Oh, Jane, really!"

"Mum, it was fine. No-one was going to look at me, were they?"

Jane could almost hear her mother grind her teeth and thought it time to end the call.

"I must go, Mum. Let's talk soon. Love you! Bye!"

Jane left her mother to shake her head in frustration at her daughter, and went back to her own morose musings.

After Felicity dumped her she had been quite physically ill with grief. It came just as she had been brave enough to be totally open with her, about her love and her needs, and express the joyous wish they could make a life together.

But Felicity seemed annoyed, even amused in a cruel sort of way that Jane had invested so much into their affair. She said she'd only gone to bed with her to find out if she was gay, and what being made love to by a woman felt like. She was now going back to her husband and their very comfortable life, thank you very much. And no way was she ever coming out.

That pain felt like a knife in the gut, or more appropriately, a bullet in the back, but it hadn't been depression like this. The trauma she felt at Felicity's hands sent her battered and bloodied into celibacy, but it wasn't ever as bad as this energy-sapping, exhausting feeling of meaninglessness that she currently felt.

Jane tended to despise illness in herself and in others, and was a strong believer in self-care and keeping fit. Even poor Isabel, who eight months before, had broken nearly every major bone in her body, had had to endure her brisk encouragement to just stop moaning and get back on her feet. And any girls at her school who tried to dodge PE lessons by citing period pains or headaches had generally received pretty short shrift.

But now, even as Isabel suggested she look for a new partner and nudged her towards welcoming someone new in her life, Jane knew she was in deep trouble. She was intelligent enough to admit she wasn't well, either mentally, emotionally or physically, and she realised she wasn't going to shake the malaise off by simply signing up to a website.

On the other hand, it was the end of an exhausting term. All teachers felt shattered this time of year. She would take the holidays to rebalance her life and catch up on her sleep. She would recover. She'd surely soon be OK.

Jane turned off the television. In her distracted state, she was having trouble making sense of what the various commentators were saying, so she switched out the lights and went towards the stairs. She saw her bag of golf clubs propped up at their foot, and that gave her some comfort.

Over the holidays, she could play golf every day if she wanted to, weather permitting, and the idea of walking the full eighteen holes of a course, and lowering her handicap even further made her feel happy. The row of cups on her sideboard was evidence she was a very good golfer and an enthusiastic player. In the last fifteen years she'd been Ladies Captain at her golf club twice, and she held the position again now, although she found the social demands on the role far more tedious than just having to organise fixtures and pairing players up for matches.

Something about the game of golf, about the act of whacking a tiny ball 400 yards or more into a hole scarcely bigger than itself, filled her with a huge sense of achievement. Discipline and focus were the way to do it! Keep your eye on the ball, and don't get distracted.

Jane decided a few good games of golf were the obvious way out of her glums, rather than bothering any doctor for anti-depression tablets. If the weather stayed reasonable over the next few days, she would head off to the golf course.

That was the obvious solution to all her ills. She tried to convince herself that her breakdown in London had been just a one-off blip, and a few good rounds in single figures above par would restore her to her normal happy self.

In her bedroom, she slipped out of the wedding outfit...the one she had worn for her youngest brother's wedding five years before, and which her mother had derided...and hung it back up in the wardrobe, where it would undoubtedly stay for a few years more.

Jane drew her bedroom curtains against the winter night, and began to strip off the rest of her clothes. She glanced quickly at her body in the mirror. It didn't disappoint, in the sense that she still looked toned and fit, and her abs and pecs did her credit. She had broad swimmer's shoulders, and a runner's leg muscles. And she wasn't at all heavy for her 5' 9''. Physically, she was OK.

But she didn't think her face would win her any prizes. People said she had nice eyes, but she reckoned her looks were pretty ordinary, and her short blond hair was so straight and stiff, it stuck up like toothbrush. 'Bris' or 'Bristles' had been her nickname as a kid, which hadn't been very nice.

She guessed she looked like any lesbian woman in her forties, instantly recognisable as gay. She'd never been able to tantalise people and leave them guessing, as Isabel always did. She thought she looked anything but fascinating. She was an open book and as boring and easy to read as a club fixture list.

Jane sighed, and pulled on her pyjamas. Isabel's words kept coming back, try as she might to forget them. "Go and find the love of your life. She's probably out there somewhere waiting for you."

She went into the bathroom, washed and cleaned her teeth, and used the loo, and then crawled under her warm down duvet into her bed. It was a double bed, but one half was always redundant, and she turned the mattress regularly to even out the use. No-one had ever shared it with her since she'd bought it a decade earlier. Felicity preferred hotels.

Suddenly this fact made Jane feel very, very sad. Why was she stuck here in her self-imposed isolation? Why couldn't she, like Isabel, find her one true love?

The same overwhelming sense of grief and loneliness which had hit her at the wedding crawled up inside her again, and as she turned out the light, Jane was horribly afraid she might cry herself to sleep. All in all, going to Isabel's wedding had been a truly miserable experience.

Chapter 4

Home Alone Two

The next morning as Jane struggled awake to the radio alarm at 6 am, and despite the day being dark and wet, things looked a little more positive, as they tend to do after an especially hard day. Jane cursed as she realised she'd not reset the alarm from workday mode, but it wouldn't have made much difference. Her inner body clock was an accurate little machine ensuring she rarely slept late.

She hauled herself up, wrapped the blue velour dressing-gown which her mother had given her last Christmas, around herself, and found her slippers beside the bed. Then she went straight downstairs to put the kettle on and make tea. The rain was heavy outside on the close and she could hear traffic on the nearby main road beginning to move.

Jane remembered her first sight of Isabel's little holiday cottage in mid-Wales from the time she'd visited back in late July, and thought how quiet and peaceful it would be right now.

She could imagine Isabel and Bryony getting up to goodness knows what on their honeymoon, and smiled slightly, pleased she'd been part of the large group of wedding guests to wave them away at the end of the reception. They had been planning to return to the Welsh hillside where they'd met, and she supposed they had enjoyed a night of high passion and some deep and sweaty sex in the woods north of Machynlleth.

Bryony, the young medical student Jane had dismissed as a mere infant when she'd first met her, obviously possessed more pizzazz inside her that she'd realised. Bryony had captured Isabel's heart, hook, line and sinker. Crazy, brilliant, battered Isabel was now happily married Isabel. She was no longer the wild heart-breaker Jane had known for thirty years, but now, someone tucked up in a sickeningly perfect love-nest!

The kettle boiled, prompting Jane to brew tea in a large mug. She sat down at her kitchen table to make a list. There was a lot to do. Her first task was to go into school and to finish clearing all the work she hadn't been able to finish on Tuesday.

Many of her colleagues would have done this yesterday, but of course she'd been in London. In about two hours, Jane would do a quick sort-out of her files, records and timetabling schedules, catch a quick meeting with some of the other department heads, and maybe throw out a load of redundant papers which had accumulated on her desk.

Jane was generally professionally organized and efficient, and rarely behind with her marking. During the school holidays she often organized extra coaching practice, but not this time of year. The Christmas vacation would be blessedly free of kids, free of worrying about the spring fixtures, free of everything school-related. After all she was a woman as well as a teacher, and she had two weeks in which to reclaim her life.

At home, Jane found domestic duties intensely boring, but there were other little tedious jobs to complete, Christmas cards for starters. She hadn't had time to buy any yet, let alone write them.

Adamantly non-religious and always happy to declare herself an atheist to anyone who bothered to ask, Christmas held little meaning for her. But she did like the lights and the warm silliness of the whole thing, and when her brothers' children had been small, she'd enjoyed seeing them play with their toys and squeal with delight at the thought of Santa coming down the chimney.

Her nieces and nephews were by now in their early teens though, and cash or gift tokens were always more welcome than anything from a toyshop. It made Christmas shopping much easier, if rather sterile.

Her mother though, who was definitely expecting her to visit and stay in Cheshire with her as usual for ten days or so, still liked proper presents, so she factored in a trip to the vast shopping complex, Cribbs Causeway, near to Bristol on the M5, to take a quick look around the department stores there.

M&S would probably be the one where she'd end up. It was her mother's favourite store where she liked to worship at each counter like a shrine to St Michael, the patron saint of boring. It also gave her the chance to return whatever sweater or slippers her daughter made the mistake of buying her.

Jane wondered why she just didn't give her mum a gift token in the first place, but the old habits of her adult life were hard to alter, especially at Christmas. She was very fond of her mother, who had always accepted her daughter's sexuality from childhood, and gave her more support than many of her friend's parents did to them. She just knew her mother hoped she'd find a lasting relationship with someone who would be worthy of her, and the continual interrogations about new acquaintances did get tedious, year after year.

The tea was hot, good and consoling. Jane scanned her list of jobs she planned to accomplish over the next few days, including cleaning the cooker, sorting out the garden shed, and booking her Rav4 in for a service. She could do these things in the morning, and then play golf from noon onwards, before the light faded on the Course. She wrote at the top of the list, 'book Tee off slots', and that cheered her up a little. She'd also call some of her golfing girlfriends to see if they would like to partner with her, even though most of them would be tied up with family or Christmas preparations.

But, but…nothing on her list looked remotely interesting, not really. Nothing in the next two weeks sparked her imagination, or warmed her soul. Jane felt like she wasn't living at all, wasn't in anyway enjoying a real life and being the real woman lurking inside her. Why did everything in her world seem as dry and as dusty as some desert landscape? Why couldn't she be happy?

She finished her tea and pulled herself up from the table. There was only one thing to do, something she did every morning of her life, and which never failed to improve how she felt. Jane decided to disregard the cold, dark December dawn, and go pounding out around her nearby suburbs for a five mile run.

But first she added something new to her "To do" list, -

Apply to lesbian dating site. There it was, in bold red marker pen, and she decided to follow through with it. After all, what did she have to lose?

Chapter 5

Not Working Nine to Five... More like Eight till Seven

When Isabel let herself back into the Righteous Anger office on January 3rd, 2020, after her curtailed honeymoon and various other adventures, she pulled up the blinds and opened up the windows to clear the air. She had arrived alone, a full hour before any of her colleagues, and relished the chance to get a head-start on a new year and face new challenges.

She sat down at her CEO's desk in the furthest corner and started to put in place the plans she had been hatching over the previous two weeks. She resolved to make 2020 the year Righteous Anger really met its funding targets and achieved its goals, but to do this, she needed to move fast.

Steph Hunter, her senior Programme Manager, had just given her notice to leave, for perfectly laudable reasons, which Steph had communicated to her while they had met in Brussels for the New Year. Steph was going to marry Alana, the one true love of her life, and move with her to New York in the early spring, so Isabel needed to appoint someone fresh to the team, someone who could manage at least half of Steph's portfolio of street children and education projects, and who knew her way around the politics of West Africa. And Isabel thought she might have found just the right person.

In addition the Conservative Party victory in the recent General Election had endorsed the Brexit referendum. If her worst fears came true, it would be catastrophic for a small charity like RA, as the result threatened to scupper any future European funding which currently supported half their projects in Africa.

It was Isabel's job as the CEO to make sure the agency had a viable future, and the best plan she had was to merge with a smaller, more specialist agency, and to bring in their supporters under the same umbrella as well.

She picked up the phone and called the most recent number she had added to her contact list in Brussels. Was it too early to call? She glanced at the clock, but mainland Europe was an hour ahead, and Isabel knew her intended recipient would be up with the lark.

"Jenni? Great. Hi love. How are you? How are the girls? We miss you already. Now listen, about what we discussed...I definitely do need you here in London. How quickly can you get here? Early next week? Fantastic! Now sit down and listen. I want to fill you in properly with what I have in mind..."

In Brussels, Jenni Argent, or Sister Jennifer Marie, as she'd been known to the world for the last thirty-five years, answered Isabel's call while she was sitting in a local bar. When it finished, she flicked shut her phone to save its battery, and gave a small smile of relief. A new day, a new year, and possibly a new life lay ahead.

She was perched on a stool at the counter, using the bar as a makeshift Internet café, to catch up with her emails and enjoy a fresh coffee. The bar-owner followed her hand gestures, and pushed a second tiny cup of espresso over towards her, which she swallowed in a single gulp. Caffeine was bad for her kidneys, but she didn't care. It helped sharpen her mind.

Jenni was in the European city on a mission. Her whole life seemed to have been defined by that potent word. But this mission had been more important and potentially more dangerous than most.

Leontine, a young AIDS orphan she had supported from infancy in the Democratic Republic of Congo, had been abducted from school in early December and trafficked to Europe, intended for the savage world of enforced sex-work.

Luckily, Steph Hunter's quick thinking after she had encountered the child on a flight from Kinshasa the week before Christmas, had enabled them all to save her, along with another teenager from Nigeria. Jenni, who was unwillingly on retreat in Canada, had jumped on a plane and arrived in London on December 26th. She brought Steph and Alana with her to

Brussels to track down the traffickers and rescue the girls, who had been released from hospital into her care.

Jenni was in *loco parentis,* and was still helping the fifteen-year-olds find sanctuary in the strange city. She had been able to bring Leontine and Patience, the shy and frightened African teenagers, back with her from hospital to stay with her in her friend Sophie's small apartment.

Sophie, as a lay-woman, had taught with Jenni in the same Mission school near Goma in the DRC, for more than ten years. Sophie had impressed on her that her 5th floor apartment could be a home for her and the girls for as long as they needed it. She had such a warm and generous spirit, and admitted she craved company.

Both women spoke fluent Lingala and Swahili, and Jenni knew if she left Leontine and Patience under Sophia's protection, they would have the best care, even though the case in which they were key witnesses might not come to trial until the summer. So Jenni's first job as the new academic term opened was to enroll the girls into a good Brussels secondary school, and restore some sense of routine and normality to their lives. This was her task for the morning.

The girls were currently sleeping upstairs in the top-floor flat, still pretty traumatised by the abduction and imprisonment they'd endured, and Sophia had left early to take the tram to her job in a UN Migrants Agency. So Jenni, restless as ever, had come out for an early morning walk around the block, to sniff the brisk frosty air, and read her emails over a perfect few millilitres of coffee.

For decades her daily routine had included an hour of quiet prayer and meditation in the early morning, which, back in Africa, would have been followed by compulsory attendance at a daily Mass in the school chapel. The routine had carved a groove in her psyche. Now, even though everything in her life was in flux, she still craved time to be alone, even if it was in a cosy and slightly grubby city bar over too strong coffee and a croissant.

This unexpected adventure, if she dared call it that, had come at just the right time. It broke into a period of deep spiritual crisis for her, and had successfully deflected from her having to spend any longer in the austere surroundings of the convent in Quebec.

She rang Sophie, who was already at work. They nattered together in French, and then Jenni broached the big favour she was about to ask Sophie for.

"Hi, Isabel has just phoned me and offered me a job, temping as a programme manager in her charity. I can start on my tourist visa and then she may be able to get me a work permit."

"Fantastique! Just what you need…"

"Yes, but the girls. It's so much to ask, but could you consider looking after them?"

"Say no more, Chérie; it will be my absolute pleasure. They are lovely girls, and no bother. And you'll be back for the trial, won't you?"

"Wild horses couldn't keep me away. But I'll be back before that. I'll come over to Belgium in March, for the end of their semester, and give you a break. I could take them to Bruges or Paris, give them a little holiday."

If she could get the necessary immigration status, Jenni hoped she would be able to move from Brussels to London and perhaps work in England permanently. This would mean she wouldn't have to return to the severe and gloomy convent which was her religious order's mother house near Montreal. She could also get a reprieve from dealing with the secret inner turmoil which had been growing in her head for at least fifteen years.

Jenni, who had entered the religious life before she had even left her teens, had naively signed up to become a life-long bride of Christ at twenty-one. She'd still been only a sophomore at Boston College at the time, and was barely half way on the path to becoming the qualified French and English teacher her Superiors needed her to be.

Theirs was a missionary order, and they urgently needed replacement teachers for their schools in Africa. Sending her south to the USA to take a degree in modern languages, while keeping a tight grip on her social life in their own hall of residence in Boston had worked wonders for ensuring Jenni conformed to the model of an ideal nun, and was too busy to have many of her crazy flights of fancy or rebellious episodes.

That was thirty years ago though, and these days Jenni was older, and wiser. She had fought many battles with God and the Church and her heart bore the scars.

The new hopes and promised reforms in the Catholic Church had never been truly transformative, and the forces of conservatism...and even worse...of corruption, seemed impossible to shift. Women could still not be ordained, which was quite ridiculous in 2020, and the current Pope Francis seemed to be a voice crying in the wilderness.

Many of her best friends and former closest associates had already quit the Order and the Church, and kept urging her to do the same. She felt she was stuck in a loveless marriage to which she had given her heart and soul.

And much more importantly, while she fought many battles with the hierarchy, Jenni's God had also abandoned her...simply walked out on her, floating away in silence and leaving her to sort her own life out. Her many prayers had been met by a blank wall of seeming indifference, or at best, a continual spiritual 'busy signal' on the line.

The nastiest little sting in the tale though, was that Jenni had been given a special farewell gift, a chronic condition of the liver, caused by repeated attacks of malaria, which meant that she could no longer work in Africa, and was dependent on little white pills to keep her alive.

Africa was her home, her beloved continent, her life-long passion, and it was now barred to her. If she returned to live and work anywhere south of the Sahara she was told she would undoubtedly die.

Three months previously, Jenni had been exiled from all she held dear and precious and she was effectively made redundant on health grounds, and was told to immediately leave the girls' high school she had led for decades. She'd been welcomed back to Canada, as sympathetically and as warmly as her community knew how, but they could see as well as she did, that she had long outgrown institutional life, and she would only cause trouble if she stayed.

Essentially the governing Council, led by the local Archbishop, had said to her they would fund her to do whatever she wanted, as long as it could be deemed useful and on the side of the angels. They offered a separation, and hoped she wouldn't make it a divorce. They even gave her a credit card, with a very generous amount to spend if she needed to. So what was done was done. All she could do now was to make the right choices in future.

In 2020 white missionaries in Africa, or anywhere else, were by and large seen as dinosaurs. Her successor as Principal of the High School was a young, dynamic African woman with bright ideas. And what could a fifty-year-old woman in less than perfect health offer the world? Who was she anyway, to think she had any wisdom or experience to offer?

All these questions, Jenni had been struggling to answer, but now, out of the blue, Isabel was giving her a whole new sense of direction. Her skill-set was perfect for working in development for a small NGO. This, in addition to her ability to rough it and little need in the way of personal compensation, meant that she was as free as a bird.

For the first time in ages, Jenni felt a decided spring in her step. She paid for her coffee, slipped her tablet back in the leather messenger bag across her shoulder, and pushed her fingers through her mop of pepper and salt curls. The weather was cold in Brussels, but not as cold as it had been in Quebec, and she zipped her jacket, flung her borrowed scarf around her neck several times and pushed her fingers into the pockets of her battered leather flying jacket.

She didn't have to go back to the convent she mentally nicknamed *St. Gloomsville*. She didn't have to swallow every natural instinct and obey the endless little rules imposed there by a Mother Superior young enough to be her daughter, and if God chose not to talk to her, then she could return the favour.

Jenni stepped out from the café into the busy Brussels streets and went to find the nearest Metro station. She would settle her young charges in school, assure them of her unflinching support until they could return to Africa, and then she would check the time for the Eurostar trains to London. She felt ridiculously free and yes, almost happy again!

Chapter 6

Don't Ask, Don't Tell (So boring!)

In Chester, where all Jane's immediate family still lived, the Christmas period slid by smoothly, and Jane found her very low expectations of a happy holiday were actually exceeded. Her mother had received her without further wistful hints about Jane's permanently single status. Her two brothers each gave her a good round of golf at their local club, (where she was easily able to thrash them both), and her sisters-in-law as usual, pleasantly avoided any personal conversations with her at all.

Their reticence was totally as expected, so it didn't remotely surprise her. Even after the many years since she had come out as a gay woman, her siblings still seemed to follow the old American military mantra of '*Don't ask. Don't tell.*'

Jane did sometimes wonder what on earth they thought she was getting up to, down in the fleshpots of Bristol! Did they secretly imagine she was having wild sex with bus-loads of different women? Part of her rather hoped they might.

She couldn't bear the thought that they would pity her because they knew just how empty and boring her personal life really was. But in her mother's house, she had company, and there was good food, small talk, TV specials, and far less opportunity to sit down and feel self-pity.

Anyway, she at least made it through the holidays without breaking down again. Her mother genuinely seemed to like the pretty cardigan and blouse she'd given her and had not even quietly asked her for the receipts so she could pop them back to Marks and Spencers as soon as the holidays were over. That seemed a minor personal triumph in itself!

On the four-hour drive back to Bristol shortly after New Year's Day, Jane felt relieved the break had all gone so well. She settled back into her plain little townhouse, 27 Cropton

Close, opened her lap-top and eventually looked again at the on-line dating site, *Her Space*, which she had decided on as her best option.

Her Space seemed user-friendly enough, and the costs of joining as a basic subscriber were minimal, so she bravely started the procedure filling in an application. After the first few questions though, she had to stop and brew some hot, strong tea before she felt brave enough to continue. This was scary stuff!

To begin with, there was a multiple-choice questionnaire she was supposed to complete, and she was given so many different options to describe her rich and glorious life, and her many talents and interests, that she was initially floored.

There were all sorts of personal questions, some of which she felt were quite intrusive. And then there was the million dollar question. What sort of person was Jane Walkley really looking for? Who would be her one true love? To be honest, she hadn't a clue.

Age bracket? Well, the same age or older for a start. Jane didn't want to chase twenty-year-olds with strange idioms and texting shorthand she wouldn't even understand. She also wasn't at all into tattooed sleeves or purple hair. Shaved heads were out, as were piercings. She shuddered at the thought. So, her fingers hovered over the keys and she put in *40-55*. Well, that was a start at least.

She took a swig of tea and pressed on.

Educational level? How rude! She wasn't an intellectual snob, but as she scanned down the options, she felt she had to be honest, and ticked the *Master's* box. She did have a Master's degree in Education after all, and a veritable crowd of post-grad certificates in various forms of sports science, management, coaching and careers counselling.

Then things got trickier. The site's computer wanted to know all about her interests, what excited her and what made her tick.

Jane began by listing all her sports, at least the ones she played to county level; *golf, hockey, cricket, swimming* and yes, she supposed, tennis, (even though the Felicity Fellows experience had meant that she had not picked up a racquet for pleasure for at least twenty months afterwards.) Then she reconsidered and decided to go back and erase the word *tennis*. No way was she ever dating any tennis player again in this life!

But the form nudged her forwards. Besides sports? What else could she claim as an interest?

Jane went down the various suggested categories. *Animals* – no, she had never kept any animals. Dogs were always ridiculously slobby and dependent, exuding all that false cupboard love and pretending you were their best friend, even if you were a perfect stranger.

She secretly admired the grumpy "Up yours" attitude of cats, but suspected she might well be allergic to their fur. Horses rather scared her, and farm animals in general worried her with their staring unknowability. She preferred to just think of them as something potentially on the plate, not as people, even though Isabel was a new convert to vegetarianism, and had tried hard to make her become one too.

Country Pursuits? Well, she enjoyed a walk as much as the next woman, but relished it even more if there was a little white ball to chase along the way. She had never been a rambler. Nor was she a shooter, angler, or an orienteering exponent.

When she was young, her happiest memories were connected with membership of the girl-guides, camping and going on expeditions, but that was rather too connected with the crush she'd had on an attractive young Guide Captain with long brown legs, who had once taken her camping to Guernsey for two weeks. She could still tie knots like a pro, and build a mean camp-fire. But that was about it as far as the great outdoors went.

Politics and current affairs? - No, the current long drawn out misery over Brexit had stopped her listening to most of the news on the television. She reckoned Isabel would tell her if the end of the world was imminent, and she always contributed to the seasonal appeals by UNICEF and the UNHCR, but she couldn't begin to grasp the complexities of globalisation, or even climate change. Nothing to put there then!

Travel? Adventuring? - Maybe once, but the only trips she

had taken in the last five years had been to follow the English women's cricket team, and annual holidays with her mother in the Lake District.

Jane went on through the list of all the cultural possibilities available to any normal woman, gay or straight, and realised she wasn't qualified to include herself in very many of them at all. She was an obvious philistine.

She saved her entries and sighed profoundly.

She really couldn't imagine any worthwhile woman would be remotely interested in making friends with such a boring, one dimensional person as described in this questionnaire. But she made one last effort and tried not to be so hard on herself.

The last section asked her to sum up who she was, and also where she hoped to be in five years' time.

"I'm a teacher, committed to supporting my students reach their potential in whatever field they chose to work or study. (Boring!) *In five years' time I would like to have expanded my horizons and be sharing my life with a person who can help me achieve this. I am fit and strong and have no dependency issues. I can offer loyalty, reliability, companionship and love."*

Heck, this only made her sound just like a sheep-dog looking out for a kind new home where it wouldn't get beaten! Jane scrubbed out the *no-dependency issues* phrase, which implied she was a recovering alcoholic, and instead just put in *'non-smoker'*.

Finally as she checked over the form, she saw she had missed out one last question, about *'religious affiliation'*. What religion was she? She wrote the same thing she'd done on her passport application and firmly typed *NONE* into the box.

That was one thing she could be absolutely sure of, without hesitation. Jane knew she was an atheist. She had been one since she first learned the term at the age of ten, and she certainly wouldn't want anything to do with any religious nutcases who might look at her form.

Just at that moment, the phone rang, and she saw on Caller ID that it was Isabel contacting her.

The woman's musical voice hit her ear as soon as she responded.

"Hi, sweets, how have you been doing? I've thought about

you loads over the last couple of weeks, but events rather ran away with us here in London and then Bryony and I had to go to Brussels."

Jane was more delighted than she admitted to hear from Isabel, in whose life she could vicariously experience some of the full and varied adventures which her own obviously lacked. She responded to Isabel's question and told her how she had cheered up after their last conversation, and how the trip north to Chester had panned out. It was the home-town to them both, and Isabel knew Jane's mother and her brothers from childhood, so she was interested enough to stay on the phone and chat for quite some time.

Then Jane mentioned she had decided to send in her profile to the *Her Space* website and see if she could connect with some other lonely lesbians out there.

"Wow, well done you! I'm proud of you. Are you going to let them see a photo?"

Jane gulped. "No, not at first. Supposing some of my students went on there and saw me. It would be mortifying. I'll wait until I connect with someone on a person to person basis, and then reveal my identity. I'm sure you can do it like that."

"Well, choose a good pseudonym then. Jane, you are an attractive, warm and enthusiastic person with heaps of talents. I'm sure there is someone just right out there in the world that is waiting to be your soul-mate."

Jane knew Isabel was partial and prejudiced in her favour, but her kind words still cheered her up. Then she wanted to hear all about the honeymoon and what her friend has been doing since.

"We had to come back to London early, as Bryony was called in to cover over the Christmas holidays. She's now doing a placement on the Accident and Emergency Unit at St. Thomas's and will be there for the next six weeks. This final year before qualification is pretty intense for her, but she's coping so well. She wants to specialise in orthopedic surgery afterwards, so I expect she'll be in training for years to come. I'm very proud of her.

"But, Jane, how's this for exciting news? We have had a

real breakthrough in the hunt for Carrie's murderer! Interpol thinks they have identified the man who shot her. That was why I went to Belgium, to hand over my files to the police there. And while I was there I met up with someone I worked with years ago in Africa. It was great to see her again, and we are applying to get her a visa to join us at Righteous Anger."

Jane heard the smile in Isabel's voice, and was happy for her. It was great that there was justice in sight for the murder of Bel's previous adored partner, the talented, if reckless Italian film-maker Carrie Monterini, who had been killed by people traffickers in Moldova three years before. She was still digesting this information while she responded to the second half of the message.

"Oh, yes? Someone in Africa? Would I know her?"

"No, I don't think I ever mentioned her to you. She's a French-Canadian nun, Sister Jennifer Marie…"

Jane's mind switched off into neutral, or even reverse, immediately. The very word 'nun' sent shivers up her spine, and she lost all further interest. She effectively cut Isabel off and changed the subject promptly back to her dating site application struggles.

"So, do you think I should send my entry in to *Her Space*? It makes me sound just about as boring as an empty cardboard box."

Isabel chuckled. "Don't be such an idiot. Send it in, pay the money, and wait for Miss or Mrs. Right to come whizzing into your life. Do it now!"

"Yes Ma'am." Jane promptly followed her advice. After all, even empty cardboard boxes deserved to be loved. She hoped Isabel was right. Surely somewhere in the world there might be a woman for her, someone whom she could fall for, and who might put up with her in return.

She knew the dating website had followers all over the globe, even in Australia and New Zealand. Jane decided no effort would be too great to find that elusive soulmate, and having once set her mind on something, she never normally faltered or lagged. In fact she'd go and check that her passport was up to date straight away! Maybe her new life lay just over a far horizon.

Chapter 7

A Scarf of Many Colours

Sister Jenni was on the move within a few days of her conversation with Isabel. She took her two charges shopping to kit them out with warm winter clothes and shoes for school, and also left Sophie with three hundred euros to cover their food and other necessities for the next couple of months or so. Now, on her final morning in Brussels she was packing her scanty collection of clothes into her haversack.

As she did this, Sophie presented her with a most unusual and quirky present, but one which amused and pleased her, as it would be something to keep her restless hands steady. It was a large paper carrier bag of small balls of leftover wool, in a riotous mix of bright colours, along with a sturdy pair of wooden knitting needles.

"Remember how you and I used to sit and knit together in the evenings in the teachers' house in the Congo? I recall how you found it very calming. Well now, while you are on a train or waiting for a bus in London, you can knit yourself a lovely long scarf, my darling Jenni. I know how you love bright colours, and this bag of wool has been sitting around in my flat for ages."

Jenni laughed out loud, and accepted the gift gladly. She could indeed do with something like it to keep her amused, and a warm merry scarf was just what she needed. She barely had more than the clothes she stood up in, which were a weathered pair of old blue jeans, a couple of flannel shirts, a blue sweatshirt with the convent logo, and her beloved, but battered, leather flying jacket.

Steph and Ally had given her a pair of warm gloves and a hat when she stayed with them, but she really needed a new working wardrobe, and maybe some better winter boots.

She arrived back in London on the Eurostar express late the same afternoon, five days after Isabel's phone call. Her tourist visa was good for three months, and her *Religious* status under profession raised few eyebrows.

At Righteous Anger they all welcomed her warmly and agreed she should stay for a few weeks with Trixie and her family, who lived in a tall terraced house in Stoke Newington. Jenni felt immediately happy to be back in a joyous home full of West African culture, the smells of traditional cooking, along with a bottle of hot pepper sauce on the table and the sound of the laughter of little children permeating the house.

Francis, or 'Frankie', Nabieu was a well-paid banker, so Trixie could work in the voluntary sector without being too anxious over paying the bills and they clearly appreciated how lucky they were. The ten-year civil war in Sierra Leone which had only ended in 2002 had brought both of them to England as refugee children, so they were first generation Brits.

Krio was the main language spoken in the home, but Trixie's children were definitely as British as they were African. The family made Jenni very welcome indeed, and helped her ease back into full-time English speaking, and the little quirks of British life.

She was so happy to be with a family, not exiled into a lonely bed-sit or institutionalised Catholic hostel, and it warmed her bones and her soul.

Religion wise, the Nabieu family were all enthusiastic Baptists, but their church-going seemed merry and bright, and their version of the Almighty sounded a surprisingly matey deity who was deeply involved in their lives on a daily basis.

Jenni soon grew to love them all, and especially admired Trixie with whom she travelled to work on the bus each morning. The woman was completely committed to ending FGM, and Jenni did all she could to support her in her work.

Life in the RA office was equally new and very stimulating. The office accommodation was obviously not big enough for their needs, but everyone on the staff knew the extortionate price per square foot for office space in central London meant they couldn't justify moving, so they squashed in together and hot-desked when necessary.

Festus, the finance manager, explained to Jenni how tight the budgets were. She could see how Isabel, whose natural talents and inclinations lay as a campaigner and strategist, had to devote far more time than she wanted to on fundraising, even though she was ably assisted by Caroline.

Jenni's responsibilities soon became clearer to her, as Stephanie, still euphoric with happiness over her engagement to Alana, passed file after file over to her, and briefed her on all the current projects which needed monitoring and supporting. There was a pile of overdue reports to funders which Steph had let build up while she'd been absent, and Jenni spent her first two weeks virtually chained to the desk, writing and sending reports, and clearing the backlog.

The desk she shared with Stephanie was very cramped, but the younger woman usually let her take the space as she was simply working out her notice.

Rumors of merging with a smaller charity in Bristol was a live topic between Isabel and the Chair of the Board, and Jenni was drawn into it. The Board meeting set for late January would need a full report, and one morning in the third week of the month, they both descended on Jenni and asked if she would go to Bristol to do an evaluation of the agency.

"You'll need to spend a couple of days there and come back with your reasoned assessment of whether a merger would be a good idea," said Isabel.

"I'll set it all up for you,"

She added. "They will expect you, and I've already discussed with them the possibility of our forming a new partnership with them. Their whole remit is girls' education in sub-Saharan Africa. They have four projects, two in Francophone countries, and two in English speaking ones.

"They definitely need a new director who is bi-lingual, and who can also speak the relevant African languages. This trip only requires two days, but I am wondering if we might spare you for longer, if we decided to make the partnership more formal. Will you go?"

"I'm pleased you have such faith in me, but shouldn't you

be going to Bristol to assess this for yourself?" Jenni asked.

Isabel shook her head. "No, I have to stay here. There's too much to do."

But then Isabel said something unexpected. "Oh, and don't worry about somewhere to stay. My friend Jane will put you up. You'll like her. She's a teacher like you, and she lives just a mile or two from the city-centre. I'm sure she'll be very happy to have you stay with her."

Jenni took her at her word. Any friend of Isabel's had to be a good person. But part of her secretly would have preferred a night in a Travelodge. She would have liked to have met this person, Jane, socially first before simply turning up on her doorstep demanding a bed.

"OK, but you will clear it properly with her first, explain it will only be for one night and I can easily stay somewhere else if it's the slightest trouble, won't you?"

"Of course, I'll call her tonight, and get her to text you the address and her phone number. Are you free to take the trip tomorrow? We need to crack on with this. Stephanie can do some of her own paperwork for a couple of days while you're gone!"

Jenni caught the late bus home to Trixie's place in Stoke Newington. She normally pulled out her bag of knitting for the forty-minute ride and enjoyed seeing how her multi-coloured scarf was growing day by day, but this evening she noticed a copy of Metro, the free newspaper, on the seat next to her. She picked it up and read the main article about the new Corona virus which was emerging in China.

Jenni had painful first-hand knowledge of how viruses could spread and devastate communities, in her case, of Ebola in West Africa. Her face grew sombre as she read the latest about Corona. Her bus, like nearly all in London, was crammed with people, half of whom were sniffing and coughing with various winter bugs, and she could see how quickly a virus like this new strain could sweep through London.

She was worried for her young African friends in Brussels. They would have zero immunity to even the normal European flu bugs, and she decided to phone Sophie and the girls that evening to see how they were, and to tell them she'd be away on the road for a couple of days.

Tomorrow she would be in Bristol, a hundred and twenty miles to the west of London. It was a city quite new to her.

England in general was a completely new country for Jenni to explore. She had never been able to take vacations like a normal tourist, and she was interested and intrigued as to what the city might be like. She decided to *Google* it if she had time, of course, between doing her laundry, packing her bag and reading up about the *Girls African Schools Project*, or *GASP* as the prospective new charity was unfortunately tagged.

Jenni only hoped the name wasn't indicative of the state of affairs for them. She also wondered about Isabel's arrangements for her accommodation. She pulled out her phone, and rang the number Isabel gave her for Jane Walkley.

Jenni was slightly worried when there was no answer, and she resolved to try the next day. Isabel had doubtlessly paved the way, so there was surely nothing to worry about.

Into the Rough

Chapter 8

That One True Love...

In Bristol, Jane chased through a typically crowded early evening, having just coached a netball practice session straight after school lessons, and then attended a Golf Club committee meeting. It was only when she finally made it home at eight p.m. that she realised with a sigh of intense frustration that she had left her mobile phone recharging next to her desk in her office.

Not having her IPhone with her was doubly annoying, because she had several match fixtures to confirm with other schools across the city, and for a moment she wondered if it was worth going all the way back into school to fetch it. But then, the cold dark night and the weariness in her bones worked together to persuade her otherwise. No-one important was likely to call this evening, and even if they did, their business could wait until the following morning. She could surely survive one night without her phone.

She ran from the car quickly up the short drive into her house, and flicked on the switch for the central heating. She'd been absent for twelve hours at least, so it was good she didn't have a dog or a cat. They'd have gone crazy with loneliness and boredom stuck in the house every day alone!

The interior looked uncared for and cold. Those hyacinth bulbs she'd forgotten to plant in September, and had noticed again in December, still reproached her from the hall table now in mid-January. If she had bothered to dust any time in the last few months she's have noticed them. But she hadn't. Housekeeping never had really been her thing.

She dumped her school bags by the door, pulled the curtains in the living room together and then went through to her utility room to rummage in the freezer to find something to eat. The pickings were pretty meagre, and she knew she had to restock her supplies soon.

She had a choice between some Chinese rice thing, and an oven-ready fish pie, so she pulled out the latter and pushed it into the microwave. She had grabbed something to eat from the school canteen at lunchtime, (she couldn't even remember what), but she was almost too tired to eat. The fish pie would do for now. Jane set the microwave timer, then flopped down on her sofa and pushed away a pile of school papers and marking. She opted for her IPad instead.

Even though she would never admit it, Jane was a tiny bit excited by what it might reveal. Ever since she had sent in her application to *Her Space*, she'd been sent a steady trickle of possible new women friends who might be a match for her on more than three points of her profile.

Jane decided there must be many more dull sports-freaks lurking out there in the world than she had ever imagined. Photo after photo showed pleasant looking middle-aged lesbians with very similar looks. They all tended to have short hair, open pleasant faces and the information that they loved cats, listened to k.d. lang, read Val McDermod novels, followed women's football and liked socialising with friends.

There was just one problem. Scanning down the line of pictures felt like staring at a bunch of her golfing buddies, but no-one caught her eye. Jane was very disappointed.

Isabel had assured her she would know when she met her one true love, simply by looking. That if there was a spark of something special, then she should make a move in return. But whatever the reason, none of these ladies were doing it for her. The pinging sound of the microwave drew her attention away from the disappointing soulmate search, and she stood to retrieve her solitary supper.

When she came back to the IPad, she noticed that an email had arrived from Isabel, which was nice. She opened it to see what she had to say as she spooned the bland mush of the fish pie into her mouth straight from the plastic microwave container.

The message read *"Hi Jane, I've been trying to call you all afternoon. Lost your phone? Tomorrow, I'm sending you an overnight guest, our newest staff member, the nun I mentioned, Sister Jenni Argent. She has to be on business for us in Bristol for two days, and I know you'd love some company. She has your phone number so I've told her to call you for directions and give you an ETA. She's bright and funny, a real original. I'm sure you'll like each other. Bye!"*

Jane's mouth dropped open, and she'd suddenly lost what little appetite she had for her supper. *Sister* Jenni? No way! That damned so-called friend Bel had dumped a bloody nun of all people on her without permission. She knew how much she despised and detested all professional 'religiosos'.

And even worse, this last minute demand gave her no time to find an excuse to get out of it, nor even time to clean the place up or buy some food. Her teaching timetable the next day was packed, with no free periods, and she'd be lucky to get out of school before seven.

Jane wanted to call Isabel and give her a piece of her mind, but she was impotent without her phone. Instead, she punched back a reply on the screen.

"You've got to be kidding! Well, don't blame me if she returns to you in a body bag. As if I wasn't depressed enough before. Thanks a bunch, Bel!"

It was definitely a juvenile response, but Jane felt as though she'd had been kicked in the gut. She was normally a generous minded, civil, even kindly soul, but nuns...however 'bright and funny' they might claim to be...were her least favourite people, whether in films or books. (For if she was honest, she had never knowingly ever spoken to an actual one in real life!)

A childhood terror of those long black habits and shaved heads had simply coloured her adult prejudices. She'd once seen a black and white film on TV called The Nun's Story with Audrey Hepburn and it had made her shudder. A line of subsequent other films had then only deepened her response. She guessed she was the only person she knew to have watched Sister Act and hoped the gangsters won.

And now she had to host a nun for the night. It was just too bad! The sense of doom continued all evening until she went upstairs and poked her head around the door of her tiny spare bedroom, still pretty much as Isabel had abandoned it in September.

It definitely looked comfortless. At least for Isabel, she had moved out all the weights and the treadmill she normally stowed in there, but tonight, Jane just couldn't be bothered to do the same for an uninvited stranger.

She pulled out an old single duvet cover, sheet and a pillowcase from her airing cupboard and almost flung them across the meagre radiator to air. It was stone cold but she'd turn the heat on in the morning. No point wasting electricity on such an unwanted guest overnight.

Poor, grumpy Jane rolled herself into bed, as cross as a wasp, and then tossed and turned as she tried to figure out why Isabel had done this to her. Wasn't she miserable enough already? Had the woman no pity?

Chapter 9

Texting for Beginners

Jenni, like Isabel, had also repeatedly tried to get through to Jane by phone during the same evening, obviously without success, but her view of the following day couldn't be more different. She was brim full of optimism and the anticipation of making a lovely new English friend. Any friend of Isabel's had to be a brilliant person.

Jenni arrived at Paddington Station long before sunrise, and ran headlong into the crush of commuters coming into London. She counted herself lucky to be travelling in the opposite direction, and happily sat herself down in her designated window seat, where she pulled out her knitting. She had done more than sufficient research into GASP the night before.

Her scarf was already more than two feet long, and she could see the end result in her mind already. Sophie's bag of wool would give her one at least a yard and a half long, so she could wrap it around and around her neck and protect her throat.

Jenni knitted the French way she'd been taught by her grandmother, with one needle tucked under her arm. The simple craft soothed all her shoulder tensions and took her back to her childhood in Quebec. She sometimes wished she could return there, before the time when her world had turned dark and frightening and her innocence had been shattered. But she knew one can never go back, and this journey, through new countryside and past strange towns, was taking her into the future.

She'd asked Isabel what Jane might like as a hostess gift, and been told with a laugh, "Oh, golf balls, if you pass a sports shop. You can't go wrong with those!" So, as she left the railway station in Bristol, she passed by a store she knew would sell them and picked up half a dozen mid-price ones, along with a glossy golfing magazine for good measure.

Bristol was a bigger city than she had anticipated, and it took her several minutes studying the address on her phone satnav to decide it would be much more cost effective to take a taxi than waste time trying to navigate her way by bus to the GASP offices.

She walked over to the taxi rank, and was immediately collected by a friendly Asian guy who delivered her safely to a commercial unit on an industrial estate twenty minutes' drive from the station.

She paid the cab driver with her credit card, and then walked up the ramped concrete entry to the front door. It was almost exactly 10 am and she was due at 10.15. Not bad at all.

In the anonymous, pre-fab office, she found three people, two of whom seemed rather nervous, and they all jumped up from their desks as the doorbell jingled and she let herself in.

"Hi, I'm Jenni Argent from RA. I think you're expecting me?"

They looked at her with some astonishment, at her slim open face with its faded tan, her boots and worn blue jeans, and the bag of golf-balls she was carrying. Her vigorous crop of curls was now mostly pepper and salt in colour, muted from its original auburn as the grey was creeping in. Her eyes were grey as well, but large and fringed with long lashes.

The much older of the two women came forward confidently and held out her hand. "Jenni! It's so good to meet you. If I had thought, I would have driven into town to meet you off the train. I'm sorry you've had to find your way all the way out here by yourself."

"No worries. The taxi driver knew his stuff, and I expect we can find another one to take me onwards this evening. I have to phone though at some point and find out where I'm going. Are you Pat, by any chance?"

"Of course, how rude of me!" The woman Jenni deduced must be the Chair of the Charity's board of trustees then introduced herself properly and her companions, Jim, the part-time finance officer, and Lynne the charity administrator. They were a very small team indeed.

Lynne made coffee for everyone, and then Jenni sat down with them and spent the rest of the day quizzing them all about the charity. She was specifically interested in what their strengths and weaknesses were, as well as their goals and challenges.

It was a classic SWOT analysis. One thing which was obvious to her from the beginning was that while they were raising money and giving out scholarships for female children in Africa, the UK staff seemed totally 'white'. Not much diversity there.

Pat said, "Primmy, our previous CEO, she is from Cameroon, but she wanted to go after a PhD so has returned to graduate studies. That's why we are looking pretty non-representative of our beneficiaries right now. But our partner organisations in Senegal, Angola, Ghana and Uganda, they are all led by black women."

"Yes," murmured Jenni, "It's not always easy just from reading names on paper, to know who people are."

Lynne felt bold enough to say, "That's right. With you for example! We were expecting a nun to walk in here today!"

Jenni grinned. "And you were right. We don't all have bald heads and wimples! Times have changed somewhat since Vatican Two. I've never worn a wimple in my life. When I joined, thirty years ago, we had a more formal navy-blue uniform, but very few even wear that anymore."

"So are you still under Orders?" asked Pat, seemingly still bemused by the woman sitting next to her.

Jenni wasn't sure how to reply. She was too experienced at explaining herself not to know what Pat meant, but she was unsure how to reply honestly.

"Half and half," was her final cautious reply, "But don't worry. I'm human as well." And then she steered them back on to the nitty-gritty of the discussion.

Jenni had decided the first day's meeting should concentrate on the UK foundation, the resources *GASP* had at its disposal, and the breadth of its supporter base. Then the following day, she hoped they could explore the projects and partnerships in Africa, and the people there. If possible they might even have a *Zoom* conference with the key people in the partner countries.

They broke for lunch at one, and Pat had ordered in a platter of sandwiches and a bowl of fruit. During the short break, Jenni remembered she still had not made contact with Jane.

"Oh! I must phone my prospective host for the evening, to ask her for directions."

She tried the phone number yet again to no avail. Jenni realised the obvious thing to do was to send a text. "Hi," she started, and then wondered what to write next. *"Plse send address and what time wld be convenient to arrive. Jen."*

It was abrupt, but texting was never her forte. She decided to add, *"So lking fwrd to meeting you. Thks for invite."* She pushed 'send' and the double message disappeared into the ether.

It was in the middle of the afternoon that a text message came pinging back. There was no warm and friendly greeting in the reply. It simply stated Jane's address, and the definitely curt message. *"27 Cropton Close. Eat before you come. I won't be home before 8pm."*

Jenni looked at her phone screen and tried to spin something positive out of this communication. But it was hard to read it as anything other than a distinct brush-off. Oh, well.

"Anything the matter?" Pat asked.

"Not really," answered Jenni. "It's just my prospective host for the night. She's obviously tied up this evening so we can't eat dinner together. I'm not sure what to do."

She passed over the phone. "Do you know where this address is? I'm not familiar with the various areas of Bristol."

Pat looked quickly at the text, and raised her eyebrows. "Well, that's pretty cold." She glanced back at Jenni. If you're fancy free for supper, let's take advantage and go together to Bertarelli's for an Italian nosh-up. I'd be delighted to eat with you. It will give us more time to discuss the future of our two agencies, and their food is always very good. I can even drop you at this address afterwards. It's not far off my way home."

"Pat's right. Bertarelli's is a great place to eat. I'd have liked to come too," chipped in Lynne. "But I have to get home to my kids. Sorry."

Jenni looked into the Chair of Trustees' frank and open face and nodded her acceptance of the invitation. She lived largely by instinct and impulse, and she liked Pat. She'd just have to deal with the elusive and possibly hostile Jane Walkley later.

Her reply to the text was terse. *"Thanks. Fine. I hope to be at your place by 9pm. Plse don't go to any extra trouble for me. I will be gone 1st thing tmw. JA."*

At the end of their first day's conferencing, she and Pat left together to drive in Pat's car to the Italian restaurant, where they enjoyed heaped bowls of pasta primavera and a shared pizza Napolitano.

As they ate, they talked. Jenni wanted to know why Pat had volunteered to take on the onerous role of chair of a small struggling charity, whose sole focus was the welfare and education of girls three thousand miles away in Africa.

"I lived there for ten years, in Sierra Leone, before the civil war, when its university and hospitals were among the best in Africa. I'm a semi-retired tropical diseases specialist and I still work part-time at the hospital here in Bristol."

Jenni's eyes lit up with appreciation and understanding. "Then you've come into my life for a reason! I have recurrent malaria which has damaged my liver, and which I'm hoping to get the better of eventually. It's why I've had to leave my post and come back from DRC."

"Really? Tell me more," Pat prompted.

Jenni sketched out her health problems...the repeated exposure she'd had to a particularly malignant form of malaria, and how it still plagued her life. She described how it periodically flared up and rendered her pretty useless, wracked with fever, nausea and aching limbs, usually at the most awkward of times.

Pat was perhaps one of a handful of people in the west of England who might know what she was talking about. She quizzed Jenni about her medical history, what drugs she was on, and how often she suffered episodes.

"They were quite right to send you home," she concluded. "I presume you are having regular tests for liver and kidney function and blood tests."

"Well, not since I've been in the UK, but I went through a full medical check-up in Montreal. The worst fear I have is that the parasite damage will get into my brain."

"Hmm. Well, you must take care of yourself. The risk of serious illness should diminish the longer you are out of the malaria zones, but some people still have flashbacks years afterwards."

"I know. It's a minor thorn in the flesh. Others have much worse to contend with. But I haven't had an attack in months. So much else in my life is changing for the better right now, and if I can support projects like yours from the safety of a British office, then I feel my life still has purpose. Now then, let's talk about far more interesting things! Tell me more about you, your family and your career, Pat."

By the time they finally left the restaurant, around 9pm, they were very good friends indeed. Pat gave Jenni a welcome lift in her car across the city to Jane's housing estate, and Jenni decided she liked the folk in Bristol very much! She'd made at least one new buddy, and it was good.

She was naturally someone who thrived on connecting with people, and she usually made friends easily. Even though she did encounter definite hostility in some when they learned she was a nun, it usually soon disappeared when they cottoned on to the fact that she was human as well.

Chapter 10

Cold Comfort

As soon as she had tossed off the text message, Jane knew it would come across as a real downer, and immediately felt guilty. Even though she resented Isabel pushing this nun in her direction, she shouldn't have taken it out on the woman. If she'd rearranged a few things she knew she could have reached home earlier, and prepared something decent for dinner. If she was honest with herself it wouldn't have been impossible at all.

By the time she arrived home just after 8pm, to a cold, dusty and uncared for house, she felt even more conflicted. She should have asked how her guest was intending to find her way across a strange city to her address. She should have phoned her in person instead of texting, and then offered to pick her up.

Isabel had probably expected her to be as helpful as she could be. But because of her bad manners, the nun would now have to fend for herself and then possibly cope with an evening bus schedule which was patchy in the extreme. It was shabby behaviour and she was ashamed of herself.

But perversely, to prove to herself her text message hadn't been deceitful, Jane deliberately stayed even later than she needed to at school, hanging around the gymnasium to watch a boys' basketball game, and unnecessarily engaging her male counterparts on the staff afterwards in small talk about looking at new branding for their school sports-gear.

Unfortunately for her, Greg, her male counterpart in the sports department, shook his head and said he had to get home to his wife and kids. That left Jane to drive home alone, to face she knew not what.

The ready-made Chinese meal for one, now the sole edible candidate in her freezer, tasted as horrible as it looked, and she threw half of it away uneaten. It simply left a stale smell of dried shrimp and soy sauce hanging around the kitchen. Jane opened the last bottle of beer she found out on her counter, and took a swig. Even that didn't taste as good as it might usually have done.

Then she remembered she'd even neglected to turn on the radiator in the guest room. There would be ice hanging from the curtain rail at this rate. She galloped up the stairs and turned on the radiator, and then adjusted the thermostat on the boiler control to raise the temperature of the whole house to an acceptable level of warmth. This nun had come recently from Africa, hadn't she? Wasn't that what Isabel had said? So her blood might be thin. The spare bedroom still looked like a dumping ground, but at least it would be a few degrees above freezing.

Then, as she came back down her stairs to the ground floor, she heard a car draw up outside, and the sound of conversation and laughter ring out into the cold night.

"Thank you so much... it was all lovely...Would you? That would be wonderful. So see you tomorrow morning! 'Bye!" And then there was the sound of a door shutting, and the car reversing out of her narrow close, back the way it had come.

Jane moved like a zombie towards the front door and managed to pull it open just as the bell buzzed. She wasn't sure what she was expecting. She just had a cartoon image in her head of long black garments, and a stiff old woman in a wimple clutching a black suitcase. What she saw threw her normal powers of perception completely off course.

A strong and cheerful voice came towards her through the darkness.

"Hi, you are Jane, obviously. I'm so sorry to descend on you like this out of the blue. I'm Jenni."

Jane croaked a little as she tried to speak. "Er...yes...Sorry... I was expecting..." And then her mouth spoke of its own accord with a fatuous question. "Sorry...? Where's the nun?"

Jenni seemed to think this was a deliberate joke. She moved forwards in a friendly but somewhat assertive way, so Jane had to step back into her own hallway to let her in.

"The nun? Oh, she couldn't come. I'm here instead." And she laughed again to show she was joking. Then she thrust a small plastic carrier towards Jane with the golf balls inside along with a magazine.

"Isabel said you are a demon golfer, and that these might be acceptable as a hostess gift. I hope they're all right...not too cheap or anything. I don't know about these things."

Her accent was a charming mixture of French and North American inflections, and her face was so attractive with its half-smile and grey eyes that Jane simply stared at her. She took the bag and mouthed a "Thank-you", then came to her senses and tried to make amends for her previous rudeness.

"Come in, please and make yourself at home. I'm sorry I wasn't here to give you supper. You must be cold and tired. Let me take your jacket."

Jenni pulled off her beanie hat, revealing a tousled mop of brown-grey curls, and slipped off her battered leather flying jacket. She stuffed her hat and gloves into the pockets before she handed it over. She had a haversack over her arm and a carrier with a bundle of what looked like knitting inside, which she dropped by the stairs. Her eyes were merry and kind.

"Don't give it a thought. We went out for an Italian. I am absolutely full and couldn't eat another thing!"

"Are you sure?"

"Well, perhaps a glass of water would be welcome."

"Yes, of course." Jane knew water was something she could provide, but she was ashamed by her visitor's obvious assessment of how minimal her catering arrangements probably were. She took her leather and sheepskin jacket and hung it up in the hall. They both went back into the kitchen.

"So you've been with friends?" Jane filled a glass from the cold water tap.

"Not exactly. I was with the Chair of Trustees for the educational charity; the one Isabel is hoping to partner with. It's called GASP and I'm afraid as you say in English, that it is almost on its last gasp indeed. I've never met her before. But she invited me to Bertarelli's for an Italian meal. We have just made very good friends over dinner. We had a lovely time, so you must not worry at all about not being able to be here until now. I was well looked after."

Jane handed her the water, and immediately astonished herself by feeling a sharp pang of jealousy towards the other woman, this new friend who had literally gone the extra mile to drop Jenni off at her house. She could have been in her place if she'd been sensible. She could and should have taken this chirpy Canadian out for supper.

Now, all she had to offer was a cold bed, probably damp bed-linen, and a house which hardly looked a home. Jane did a little bit of self-assessment and didn't much like what she found. She was equally horrified to suspect she might be about to find this nun, who wasn't acting like a nun, dangerously fetching. She led her out of the kitchen through into her sitting room.

"Come over here and sit by the fire," she said. "I'll turn it on."

She picked up a pile of papers that needed to be marked, off the chair opposite her own, and gestured for her guest to sit down. Jenni took the hint and drew up as close as she could in front of the electric fire, and stretched out a pair of slim blue-jeaned legs. She sipped her water and seemed to be content to wait for whatever Jane would do next. Jane sat down in her usual chair, opposite the TV, and felt her mind turn to verbal porridge.

The woman opposite her reminded her of a charming but potentially lethal school inspector who would soon uncover all her faults and failings. Jane watched Jenni glance around the bare walls of her sitting room, and assumed she saw nothing to be impressed by. Jane just sat there in stupefied silence, not knowing how to break the ice and start the conversation.

They had an hour or so to fill before Jane could reasonably suggest they turn in for the night, and she tried to think what they might talk about. She felt like an eleven-year-old schoolgirl trying to impress a sixth-former and fumbled about for a neutral area of conversation. 'Just don't mention God!' she instructed her poor stupid brain.

After several long minutes as they listened to the clock tick around on the mantelpiece Jenni gave an almost audible sigh, and picked up the ball.

"Isabel has informed me you're a talented teacher, Jane. Why don't you tell me all about your school?"

Jane opened her mouth at last and began to speak.

Her words came out very stilted and formal, but she managed to impart a few facts about her ten-year career at Reedbridge High School and her role within it. Not only was she Head of Girls' P.E., but she also ran the careers advisory service for the older students, and arranged work experience places for all the Year 12 pupils. She carried on until she realised she was making her work sound very boring, when in fact she did love it, and poured her energies into it.

Jane stopped talking and watched Jenni scan the room and focus on all the silver cups and plaques around the sitting room.

"I see you are quite an accomplished sportswoman," Jenni said.

"Oh, a few are for tennis, but most of those are for golf. I still play competitively when I get the chance. Every game is different, even over a course you know like the back of your hand. I don't suppose you have ever played?"

Jenni shook her head. "No, never. But when I was a kid, I played tennis. I grew up in the Martina era, and we all thought she was wonderful."

Jane digested this little piece of information. Was it a code to convey the message that her houseguest wasn't as homophobic as she imagined most nuns to be? But if the woman liked tennis, that was another black mark against her.

Tennis was what had brought Felicity into her life, when she'd joined the tennis club and wheedled Jane into giving her some private lessons. To say it had ended badly was the understatement of the year. She certainly wouldn't be offering to coach the nun opposite her any time soon.

"Well, I can't imagine there was much chance to play tennis in Africa," she said coolly, and then asked, "Would you like a cup of tea before we go to bed? I do have some decaffeinated still in the cupboard, left over from when Isabel stayed with me back in September."

"That would be great. Thanks. I would like some tea.

Black, please."

And so ended Jane's first attempt at bridge-building.

Jenni accepted the mug of tea, which to be honest, did taste rather stale. But it might warm her stomach and be something to help swallow down her pills. Jane obviously expected them both to turn in for the night now, so balancing her mug in one hand, she picked up her haversack and followed her host up the narrow stairs. There were four doors on the landing.

"That's the bathroom, and the one at the front is my bedroom. Then I use the second bedroom as an office, and so I'm afraid you will be in the smaller, third bedroom where I store some fitness equipment. I haven't had time to make the bed up, but there's a feather and down duvet and the sheets have been airing on the radiator for an hour or so."

Jenni squeezed past her as she held open the door, and entered a room which reminded her exactly of the little cell she'd lived in for her first year as a young postulant in the convent. There was a single bed, which needed to be made up, and a small desk and chair. Any other available space was taken up with a set of weights and an electric treadmill. Moreover, tucked at the back was a boxer's punch bag on a spring with a weighted stand. Did Jane Walkley like to knock the stuffing out of people then? She couldn't imagine why anyone would want to waste precious moments of their life playing on such things.

In fact Jenni almost got the giggles at the austerity and complete lack of joy or comfort in the room. Thank God she'd only be here for one night. The bed was new enough at least, and she could just roll herself up in the duvet and soon nod off. In her long and varied life she had learned to sleep anywhere, even with rats scrabbling under her bed, or down on a thin mat on an earthen floor. Jane Walkley might be trying to alienate her as much as possible but she couldn't scare her this easily.

Jane said an abrupt "Good night. Sleep well," and then retreated to her own quarters.

Jenni put her mug of tea down on the desk and picked up the linen. It was hardly worth making up the bed, but she supposed she should appear half-civilised at least, so she unfolded the cotton sheet, duvet cover and single pillow case, and put them to their proper use.

Then she pulled the curtains across the small window at the end of the room, and began to undress. She sometimes slept in a Tee shirt and boxers, but England was so cold that she'd recently bought a new pair of warm, brushed cotton pyjamas which felt much cosier. She left her socks on, in lieu of any house slippers, and also to keep her feet warm, for without a doubt the room was definitely on the chilly side of freezing, just like the welcome she's received from her strange host.

Jenni swallowed the last of the tepid tea, along with a little white tablet. She rushed into the bathroom and back after a quick brush of her teeth, and then crawled into bed, pulling the single duvet as tightly around her as she could. As her head hit the pillow, her thoughts were, *Sorry Isabel, but if your idea was for me to make friends with your old mate Jane Walkley, you will be sorely disappointed. The woman hates me, not sure why, but whatever the reason, the sooner I'm out of here the better.*

Jenni was disappointed with her first impression of Jane, yet, there was something about Jane...her directness and her quick decisive way of moving...that Jenni found perversely attractive, even though her attempts at conversation had fallen flat at every turn. She was also physically Jenni's type of ideal woman, big-boned but super-fit, with sharp blue eyes and blonde hair which stuck up like a little boy's.

She could also tell Jane Walkley was undoubtedly miserable. And Jenni had always wanted to bring joy to people. It was at the very centre of her sense of vocation, and the last religious duty she was likely to abandon.

If she had been allowed to be Jane's friend, maybe they could have achieved it together. But it obviously wasn't to be. She shivered again, and then began to feel her arms and legs start to ache.

Oh no! Please God don't let it be the start of another malaria relapse! Not here of all places, and with so much on her agenda for the next day! Jenni shut her eyes and just willed herself to stay well.

Down the corridor, in her own equally chilly, but double

bed, Jane's thoughts were rather different. Her mind and her heart were similarly bewildered, and she just couldn't get her head around who and what this woman staying in her house was all about.

She went over every sentence they had exchanged, every move the woman had made, how she sat, how she looked, how she listened. None of it made any sense somehow. Her manner had been moderately pleasant throughout. She had shown no resentment at Jane's ludicrously bad manners and prejudiced assumptions. But she must have seen. She must have known.

Halfway through the conversation about her school, Jane had sensed she was being judged, which is why she had retreated even further into a formal offer of a bleak little cup of tea and a not too subtle hint they should retire. It made everything worse, because while on one level Jane had clung to her obviously misguided assumptions about modern religious life and how nuns were supposed to dress and act, on another she had in fact been strangely drawn to the one sitting opposite her.

Here, in her home, was a pretty damn near perfect prototype of her dream woman, confident, self-assured, merry and worldly-wise. She was also physically cute in the rather androgynous way Jane admired. She had very slim shoulders and hips, perky, neat breasts and long legs tucked into clumpy black boots. Her face was weathered from decades under an African sky, but the wrinkles around her eyes only added character to her face, which fell into a smile far more often than showing frown lines. And her voice…Jane could easily get addicted to that warm husky voice, with its mixture of a sexy French accent, and a Canadian drawl.

Jane feared she was in real trouble here, which was why she had tried from the moment they had met to keep Sister Jenni at arms' length. She knew this was the only answer, to hide how much she liked her. Not to do so, would be to open the door to all sorts of disastrous consequences. Because, of all crazy notions, what was the point in falling for a nun? They were so off limits, it was like chasing a golf-ball out of bounds, no, even worse, far into the rough where you'd permanently lose your ball.

If you were someone crazy enough to date a married woman, there was always the faint chance she might just one day decide to divorce her spouse and run away with you. (Unless her name was Felicity of course.) But a nun! Even Jane knew when she'd met her match.

Even without believing in him, she knew she could never win with God as a rival. She was a natural fighter, but here she'd be out-gunned from the start. Didn't nuns take lifetime, unbreakable vows of chastity, poverty and obedience? And here she was, salivating over one within minutes of meeting her. The whole thing was so pitiful she couldn't believe her idiocy.

Anyway, to avoid breaking her heart all over again, the best thing to do was to push Jenni out of the door as fast as possible the next morning, and so make sure they never met again. It took her almost until midnight to arrive at this difficult but necessary decision, but once made, she resolved to act upon it. Decision made, she rolled onto her left side, the one without her old fractured rib injury, and finally fell asleep.

Into the Rough

Chapter 11

Just What the Doctor Ordered

The best laid plans of mice and men gang aft astray, as Robert Burns would say. And with only a day or two to go before Burns Night, Jenni's and Jane's plans to get as far away from each other as soon as possible, were effectively scuppered. It was almost as if a divine intervention had taken place. If it wasn't so painful it would have been funny.

It started early on Friday morning, even before Jane's 6am alarm went off. She woke to hear Jenni being violently sick in the bathroom. It sounded really bad. She pulled her dressing-gown around her and went to find out what was wrong and if she could help. The bathroom door was half open, and she could see Jenni's slim frame clinging to the toilet cistern as she lost the contents of her stomach down the pan.

Jane's practical instincts took over and she moved forward to offer a supporting arm. Soon, Jenni's nausea slowly subsided into a final bout of dry heaving. Jane flushed away the vomit, and handed her a damp face-cloth to wipe her mouth. Jane was suddenly alarmed when she looked at Jenni's wild eyes and chalky pallor, and even more when she sensed the heat of her body through the pyjamas.

Jane placed the back of her hand on Jenni's forehead. "Jeese, you've got some temperature there. You're burning up. When did this come on? It must have been what made you so sick. Do you think you've picked up this new virus they are talking about?"

Jenni closed her eyes and shook her head. "No, don't worry. It's just the damned malaria. I get these bouts now and then. I was only saying to Pat last night how I hadn't had an attack for months. It gives one a very high fever and splitting headache. And I nearly always throw up as well. I am so sorry!"

"Nothing to be sorry for. It's hardly your fault. What can I do to help?" Jane could see Jenni was starting to shiver uncontrollably as her body sought to bring down her temperature. She pulled out a digital thermometer from the bathroom cabinet and pressed it against Jenni's forehead.

"39.9. This looks bad. It should be 36 to 37."

"I've known it go up to 42. And it might rise higher now. These attacks can go on for days. I really should go to a hospital and take some strong prophylactics, but they're not exactly a walk in the park. The cure is almost as bad as the disease. And you ache so much you sometimes wish you were dead."

Jenni swayed dangerously, and raised her arm to shield her eyes from the bright light in the bathroom.

Jane slipped her hand around Jenni's back. "Come on, we must get you back into bed. I'll call the NHS helpline if you like. Do you need an ambulance?"

"No, and I'm not sure the NHS will be able to treat me, as I'm a Canadian visitor. If we can hang on until Pat arrives – she was going to come by for me this morning – she'll know what to do. She a specialist doctor in tropical diseases."

Jane could see that even their short conversation had wiped Jenni out so she assisted her back to her bed and tucked her in. She was burning hot and icy cold at the same time. Her teeth were chattering and Jane was seriously concerned. She knew little about malaria, but she knew the dangers of a high fever.

"Do you have Pat's number? If I call her she might be able to get here even sooner."

Jenni waved her hand over to her phone, and Jane picked it up.

"What's your passcode?" she asked as a grid of little dots came up.

"The letter M."

Jane drew an M-shape in the dots and the phone opened. She easily found Pat's name as the most recently added contact and pressed it to call her number. Six a.m. was quite early to disturb someone at home, but this was definitely an emergency.

Pat obviously agreed with her, because when she introduced herself and described Jenni's symptoms, the doctor said she'd be there as quickly as she could, and would bring some medicine to help. While they waited, Jane monitored Jenni's rapidly rising temperature and was frightened she would fall into convulsions.

Jenni thrashed about on the bed, half in a delirium already, while Jane rinsed the face flannels under the cold tap until they were thoroughly chilled. Then she folded one and laid it across Jenni's forehead. This did seem to soothe her and she lay back against the pillow, which was already damp with perspiration, with her eyes shut.

Hardly without thinking, Jane caught Jenni's restless hands and held them to calm her. Sweat poured off her, and her breathing was tight and desperate. Jane said things she had no time to edit or think through. They just came out of her fear that Jenni might even pass out or die on her, here right in front of her in the narrow bed.

"Sshh! Jenni, you'll be OK. Pat will be here soon. She'll bring down your temperature and help the pain. I'm here. I'll look after you. I won't leave you. Don't worry!"

Then all she could do was wait.

When the doctor arrived, it was obvious she too was concerned. Pat had brought a phial with her, of injectable antibiotic and the strongest form of anti-malarial medicine, and also some paracetamol tablets to help with the pain and bring down the fever. She stuck the needle into Jenni's upper arm and injected the full syringe. But when she took her temperature again, she shook her head.

"Do you want to take her into hospital?" asked Jane anxiously.

Pat shook her head. "No, not at this stage, but we need to lower her temperature immediately. The shivering comes from the body going into shock to try and bring it down itself. It's like a form of sepsis. Do you have a bath-tub?"

"Yes. Next to the shower, but I rarely use it."

"Well can you run a tepid bath now, not icy cold as that will feel like she's being scalded, but just gently warmed to be lower than 35 degrees? If we can get her into it, it will help reduce her fever, and then the doxycycline I've given her will have time to kick in."

Jane went immediately to run the bath, and then rapidly flung on some clothes to dress herself while Pat sat with Jenni. When she went back to check it, the water was six inches deep and of a slightly warm temperature.

Pat joined her, swished the water about, and said, "Yes, that's just about right."

They both went into Jenni's little bedroom.

"Come here and help please." Pat, rolled up her sleeves, and pulled back Jenni's bed cover.

"Jenni, love, we need to get you in the bath. This will bring down your fever. Don't fight it. In a few moments you'll feel much better."

"No, please, no!" Jenni weakly fought them off, and groaned. She seemed quite out of it still. But with Jane's greater strength and firm grip on her shoulders, she and Pat managed to get her out of bed, through to the bathroom and then out of her pyjamas. In a different situation, Jane might have appreciated looking at Jenni's rather attractive body, but the seriousness of the moment left no time for that sort of nonsense. Instead, she acted as head nurse and together, they eased her down into the bath of warm water.

"Ow, it's freezing!" shouted Jenni, but Pat firmly held her down. Minute by minute her body stopped its violent shivering, and the fever burning through her seemed to be responding. It took ten minutes of holding her down in the bath before the crisis seemed to abate and Jenni began to resemble something like her normal calm rational self once more.

Pat pulled out the plug and they both helped Jenni up of the water. They wrapped her up in a couple of large bath-sheets Jane had pulled out of the airing cupboard and Pat took her temperature again with the electronic gun against her forehead. Her fever had lowered dramatically to just 1.5 degrees above normal.

"Let's get you back to bed straight away," Pat said. "You may have several days of this ahead, with your temperature spiking up and down, but at least, with the right medicine inside you, you shouldn't go into shock like this again."

"What would I have done without you?" muttered Jenni.

"You've been like an angel." She turned to Jane. "I'm so, so sorry Jane. I wouldn't have come at all if I had known."

Jane brushed her apology away. "No, none of that. I'm just glad you were here, somewhere safe, when you became ill. But your bed is already soaked with all the perspiration. I'm not putting you back in that room. If you can wait three minutes, I'll remake my bed and you shall go in there. The room is much more suitable anyway."

Without waiting for an argument, she went to her bedroom, whipped off the sheets and pillowcases, and made her bed up again in a jiffy with cool cotton bedclothes. Jane could move very fast when she needed to, and by the time, Pat had helped Jenni dry off her body, she returned and offered her a fresh pair of pyjamas, as well as a pair of slippers.

"I'll put yours in the wash, with the duvet cover and sheets from your bed. They'll be dry again by this evening. In the meantime you should wear these."

Jane's bedroom was much more welcoming than the little spare room had been, and Jenni didn't argue as she was bundled into Jane's larger bed and propped up on two thick and comfortable pillows. Her head still throbbed and the light from the lamp hurt her eyes, but she was so grateful to the two women around her, who had known what to do, and had even maybe saved her life.

Jenni knew she wouldn't have done well if she'd been alone in a hotel room. Pat had all the medical knowledge and access to the right drugs, but Jane's prompt action in calling her, and in helping her to take that bath had also made all the difference. She didn't lie when she had told her how grateful she was for her help.

But these episodes of malaria lasted usually for three days, and she simply couldn't impose her unwelcome presence in Jane's home for that long. Only knowing how ill she truly was stopped her from trying to dress and leave at once. She knew she hadn't imagined the hostility and forced politeness coming from the woman the night before.

It was now well past eight o'clock in the morning and Jane

and Pat were discussing how best to care for her. She heard their murmuring voices, and tried to chip in, but somehow her brain and body couldn't quite connect.

"You're a teacher, aren't you?" Pat asked Jane. And when the answer came back in the affirmative, Jenni heard Pat say, "Well dear, you should get ready and leave for school. I will stay here for the morning. And when Jenni's had a good sleep and will undoubtedly feel better, we can resume the conversation we were having yesterday about our charity. I can keep her amused with an account of our overseas projects."

"I have three free periods and a conferencing time this afternoon, so I can take a half day," said Jane. "I will pick up all the necessary food for the weekend and be home by 1pm. Then I'll take over. Will that be OK? What sort of things should I buy her to eat? And tell me what medicines she'll need."

"Hey folks," Jenni managed to call out at last. "I can't put you to any of that bother. I should try and get back to London..."

They both moved back and loomed over her.

"What nonsense," Pat said firmly. "If you want to avoid being taken straight to the hospital my girl, then you will stay right here with your friend Jane, at least until well after the weekend, and preferably in bed as well. You know how painful your arms and legs will feel, so no more nonsense about going back to London. I will stay this morning and then I will pop in and see you each day, until I decide when you can be discharged. Is this clear?"

Jenni knew the voice of medical authority when she heard it, and gave up the struggle. It suddenly all seemed too much of an effort to fight Pat as well as her illness. But Jane...Jane must be horrified. Jane who hated her before she had even met her and hadn't wanted her to come at all. That had been made so obvious.

An unexpected fear came over her as she lay in the comfortable bed of her unwilling host, and then she felt the springs shift as Jane sat down on the bed next to her, and took her hand.

"Hey, Sister, I am not a totally selfish cow, you know, despite appearances. We may not have got off to the very best start, but that was totally my fault. I want you to stay. Let me look after you until you feel completely well. Please."

"But Isabel will…"

"Isabel will never speak to me again if I don't look after her friend. And anyway, what else have I got to do with myself over the weekend?"

"Um…play golf?"

"Exactly! Have you looked out of the window? Not the best weather for the next few days. So stay put and get better. I have to go to school now, but I'll be back before two."

Jenni felt Jane's other hand gently feel her forehead and then brush her fringe of curls away from her face. She was astonished to receive a gentle first real smile from the stern woman. It was a revelation, and strangely comforting. Then Jane squeezed her fingers and released her hand.

"Get some sleep!" she whispered. And she was gone.

Pat came forward with a glass of water and two paracetamol tablets.

"Here you are, dear. These will help with the pain. Now try and do as Jane said, and sleep for a while. I'll be doing some paperwork downstairs, but I can hear you call if you need me."

Jenni swallowed the capsules and then let her aching head fall back on the pillows. Jane's navy-blue cotton pyjamas were a little large for her, but they were cool and comfortable.

As Pat turned off the lamp and left her in peace, Jenni's last thought was of contentment. Things, which could have been so bad, now didn't seem so dreadful after all. And Jane...weird and grumpy Jane...would be home again in just a few hours. She fell asleep, quietly reassured and not too unhappy with that idea.

Into the Rough

Chapter 12

Way Off the Beaten Track

"What did you have to go and hold her hand for?" Jane chastised herself as she drove her elderly Rav4 to school. "She'll think you're a complete idiot!" But the impulsive gesture had seemed right at the time, and she couldn't really regret it. She had wanted Jenni to know that she was truly sorry for her previous neglect of the most basic courtesies of hospitality.

Now that Jenni was in need of all the care she could give her, she would make up any deficit. It would be the least she could do. A strangely warm feeling ran through her as she thought of the Canadian woman, nun or not, being there to greet her when she returned home that afternoon.

The house wouldn't be cold and empty. Pat and Jenni would both be waiting there, and needing her. Being needed was something Jane so rarely felt, she had forgotten what a positive feeling it was. She pulled into the staff car-park at twenty past eight, and walked briskly past groups of students congregating in the reception area for morning assembly, with a definite spring in her step.

The morning sped by, and at noon she avoided the staff canteen. Instead, she used her lunch hour to go shopping in the nearest decent supermarket. She grabbed a trolley instead of her usual basket, and went up and down the aisles, determined to stock her fridge and cupboards with decent, organic produce for once.

Whatever Jenni normally ate, junk food wouldn't help her recovery, and anyway, Jane decided she herself had had enough of microwavable rubbish for a while. She finished her shopping by filling up with some fresh fruits and vegetables, and added plenty of citrus which was in season right now.

"Seville Oranges for marmalade—One week only!" proclaimed one notice. Jane had never made marmalade in her life. She had no clue how one might even do such a thing. But she decided on a whim to buy a kilo or two of the strange looking oranges and tossed them in with her other purchases.

A strange wave of unaccustomed domesticity suddenly swept over her. She wanted to make things nice for Jenni, even if she was only her guest for one weekend, and so before she pushed her trolley to the till, she added a large bunch of flowers to her haul. Well, that was a first! Did she even have a vase in which to display them? Then Jane remembered some empty coffee jars she had in her cupboard. If all else failed she could use one of those.

When she reached home, Pat and Jenni were chatting quietly in her bedroom. She burst anxiously through the door and asked them, "How are you? How has she been?" directing her second question to the doctor. "I came home as quickly as I could."

Jenni looked at her with a wan smile, but didn't attempt to lift her head from the pillows. "I'm better than I was when you left me this morning. But to be honest, I feel like a piece of... how would you say?"

"A piece of used string?"

"*Exactement.* A piece of the used string."

Jenni seemed to have lost the fluency in her English due to the malaria attack and Jane found this endearing.

Pat said, "I'm happy to report her fever is settling nicely, and she did sleep for two hours. I think if you could rustle up a light lunch of some sort, Jenni might eat it and also manage to keep it down."

Pat stood up, as if to depart and Jane opened the door for her. Goodness knows the woman must have her own life to lead!

But before she left, Pat turned back to Jenni. "I've tired you enough already, my dear, with all the talk of GASP projects. I am going to call Isabel this afternoon and let her know your unfortunate situation, but as far as I am concerned, I would be delighted to discuss further about the two charities combining, especially if you would consider eventually coming to Bristol to be our new CEO and running our side of things."

Jane had not been aware of the real reason Jenni had come to Bristol, so this comment was a revelation to her. She chipped in with a question.

"You mean...? We might see you back down here in Bristol on a permanent basis?"

"Perhaps. I'm so sorry," said Jenni, with a wry grin. "But it's only a very faint possibility at this stage."

"But if we offered you the post of interim director, would you accept it?" pressed Pat.

And Jenni hesitated, and then nodded, her eye on Jane all the time. "Yes, if I was lucky enough to be offered the position, I would accept. If my health allows me to, that is. You won't want to put up with any episodes like this again."

Pat took her temperature one last time. "Nearly normal! Jenni, the longer you are away from Africa, the less are these attacks likely to occur, so don't worry too much on that score. I'll be back tomorrow with another injection, and then I think you can revert to medicine by mouth. For the remainder of today and tomorrow, just rest. I am sure Jane here will be an excellent nurse."

A few moments later, Dr. Pat left, and Jane and Jenni stared at each other in a shared sense of puzzlement as to how they had arrived at this point. It looked like they were going to have to spend quite a few hours in each other's company, whether they were comfortable with it or not. Jane knew how she herself felt, but she had given strict instructions to her heart all the way home in the car.

She would care for Sister Jenni (the nun!) to the best of her ability, but with no strings attached. This would be a completely sealed and signed platonic relationship, and she wasn't going to reveal the hint of the totally inappropriate crush she had begun to feel.

Seeing the woman lying in her bed, in her best pyjamas, was already enough to make the blood rush to her cheeks. But for goodness sake, the woman was just through a physical crisis which might have left her at death's door! And anyway she knew nothing about Jenni's real life or her character, just as Jenni knew nothing of hers.

"Now then, what would you like for lunch?" she asked briskly. "I have brought some salmon fillets. I thought maybe you would prefer to have fish on a Friday?"

"You mean, like a good Catholic?" smiled Jenni, apparently finding this amusing. "That sounds good. Merci beaucoup! But only a very small portion, please. I am still remembering how ill I was this morning, and I don't want to make a mess of your lovely room."

"No worries on that score. I can bring you up a bowl in case you feel sick again. If you wait here, I will fix us both up some lunch in a few minutes, and I will eat it up here with you. I so rarely have company, it will be a welcome change."

"Thanks." The woman was perfectly civil, if subdued. Jane watched as Jenni lay back and closed her eyes.

It took Jane twenty minutes to put away her shopping, while simultaneously preparing the salmon and a small packet of rice and veg for lunch. While it was steaming, she found a vase in the back of her larder, and arranged the flowers in it, snipping the ends as her mother had once taught her.

She placed them on the coffee table in the sitting room and they immediately made the atmosphere brighter and homier. While Jenni was safely upstairs she would dust and vacuum all around down here, and put away the piles of marking and old sports magazines.

Then she made up a tray with cutlery and two plates of food on it, and carried it up to her bedroom. Jenni appeared to have nodded off to sleep again, and for a moment Jane stood in the doorway and simply looked at her.

What act of the universe had brought this stranger into her bedroom, and what demonic source had decided she could never reveal that she liked her? Jane decided, yet again, to blame God. It was just too cruel. But how could she blame God if He/She/It didn't exist? Wasn't that the truth? Being a staunch atheist was harder than one might think.

Jenni's eyes opened and she gave Jane an uncomplicated small smile of gratitude.

"Here," said Jane. "Let me help you to sit up. Lunch, such

as it is, is ready to eat." She put down the tray and then plumped the pillows and encouraged Jenni into a sitting position. Then she passed her the food and took her own onto her lap, and sat on the end of the bed. They ate in silence, and then Jenni sipped her water.

"Do you enjoy cooking?" she asked Jane.

Jane shrugged and confessed. "Well, no. I find it very boring cooking for one. I'm pretty uncivilised. What about you?"

"Oh, something like this is more of a treat than you realise after a life-time of institutional cooking. And in Africa I ate with the pupils. We had a very restricted diet as food was often scarce. But I think I might like to cook, if I was ever given the chance. I have a Frenchwoman's natural enthusiasm for the idea. But I have never had my own kitchen. That would be great, but I expect it's a dream never to be fulfilled."

"So, you won't know anything about making marmalade?"

Jenni laughed out loud. "Marmalade? You mean, like *le confiture*? Orange Jam? I don't think I have ever eaten any, let alone made it."

"Yes, to put on toast for breakfast. I bought two kilo bags of Seville oranges just now in the supermarket and thought I might make some."

Jenni's smile grew wider. "OK? Well, that sounds a challenge. Do you have any jars?"

"Jars?"

"Certainly. You will need jars, to put your marmalade in."

"Oh, damn."

Jane laughed back at her, and then said, "Maybe not such a good idea, eh?"

But Jenni disagreed. "No I can see how it is an excellent idea. Don't waste the fruit. You just need some assistance with the necessary equipment. Maybe Dr. Pat has some old jars we can use. You can find a recipe online, and I will help you tomorrow. I usually feel much better by the second day of these attacks."

They laughed together at their mutual inexperience in the domestic science arena, and Jane was pleased to see how her guest had finished the small lunch she'd made her.

"Would you like some tea or a coffee now?"

"Tea please, but no milk. The parasites in my bloodstream don't play nicely with dairy."

"Sugar?"

"Just a tad."

Jane liked the American way Jenni said 'tad'. In fact, she liked more about her all the time. But she must avoid showing it. Jenni was just a friend of a friend who happened to be in need...and she was a nun. They would doubtless be parting shortly.

She took the empty plates downstairs and started to make tea. Sister Jenni might only temporarily be grounded and captured inside her house, but Jane was determined to make her so comfortable she'd give Isabel a good report of her treatment.

She pulled her favourite mug down from the rack and made her guest a fresh cup of tea, and then made herself one as well. It was nice to have someone in the house, after all.

When Jenni had drunk the tea, Jane took the cup from her, but then stood so awkwardly by the bed that Jenni wondered what she was waiting for. Their little conversation about marmalade had completely exhausted her, and she simply wasn't up to struggling through any more dialogue simply to avoid the silence which seemed to be descending between them again.

Jane looked at her in such a strange and intense way, that Jenni felt very self-conscious and ashamed of being so vulnerable and needy. Jane was obviously a fitness fanatic who probably despised all illness and especially pathetic types like herself who collapsed with mysterious diseases at a moment's notice.

But rather than apologise yet again for being in this state, Jenni decided the best thing to do was simply to turn away onto her left side in the bed, and say, "I'm sorry. I feel like I need to sleep some more. Do you mind leaving me on my own for a few hours?"

Jane came out of her little trance and nodded brusquely. "Of course. That's by far the best thing for you to do. I'll draw the curtains and leave you in peace." And then she darkened the room and disappeared.

Jenni's thumping headache, which had lifted slightly over lunch, now returned with a vengeance, and she began to shiver again. It wasn't as bad as before, but she was glad to cuddle back down under the duvet and try to go back to sleep.

Sleep was slow to come though. Jenni's brain was still tussling with why Jane, who seemed a perfectly nice woman in all other respects, seemed to have a real antipathy towards her. But then, with a feeling colder than the shivers running up and down her spine, she decided she knew the answer.

Jane most likely had a deep and entrenched suspicion and fear of gay women! That must surely be it. Jenni knew she looked gay and had never pretended to be other than she was, but she had never expressed it overtly either and she had very sadly never had the chance to follow the inclinations of her heart.

She had doomed herself to celibacy after she'd had very intense sexual feelings for her best friend at their catholic high school. The friend had been horrified and had literally run away. There was a huge and very upsetting scene when she'd been eventually been found hiding in a corn field.

At that age, with all the indoctrination she'd been given, Jenni was sure she was going to hell, and she decided to lock herself into a prison of chastity and a punishingly austere lifestyle where once even close personal friendships were discouraged.

Over the years, of course, she'd come to her senses and had long ago stopped seeing being gay as either a sin or a lifestyle choice. She also realised how bizarre it had been for her to try to escape her sexuality by entering a community where at least a third of the women there showed signs of sharing the same preferences!

Many times over the years, other sisters had obviously been attracted to her, but Jenni had never responded. She'd simply masochistically suffered in silence. She could say in truth that she had never physically broken her vows and hoped she had never broken anyone else's heart. But she couldn't help who she was, any more than she could change her basic nature, or alter the way she came across to other people.

She guessed Jane must have suspected she was gay from hearing Isabel's recommendation, because this seemed the only credible reason for her not being comfortable with having her here. Jane must have a really strict puritanical attitude towards sex. This must be why she had frozen into ice when she'd met this boyish woman, in her jeans and leather boots, and gay mannerisms.

"Oh, dear," thought Jenni. "Poor Jane. Well, all I can do is keep any physical contact to the minimum, and just try to act straight all the time. I'll try to also emphasise how religious I am. That should allay her fears and calm things down."

She was too ill to see the fatal flaws in her hypothesis. Otherwise she might have not wandered so far off the right track. But the malaria was playing tricks with her brain, and at the time, her conclusion seemed perfectly sensible. Jenni rolled over, put the pillow over her head and went to sleep, vowing to show Jane just what a good and devout nun she could be. Why not? She could be as good an actress as the next lonely lesbian.

Chapter 13

Better Lying Down

Jane spent an hour cleaning and polishing the sitting room furniture and all the surfaces downstairs, until the house gleamed. Then she settled herself in her favourite armchair and spent the afternoon quietly marking mock exam papers, which is exactly what she would have been doing had she stayed at school. But it felt so much better to be at home, sitting in the comfort of her own front room. It was a simple pleasure she never normally enjoyed, especially not on a weekday afternoon. It was also nice to know she was not alone.

Once in a blue moon, her mother might come south to visit her, and then--like now—she would willingly sacrifice her bed for her visitor. But even that was a rare occurrence...increasingly so, as her mum grew older, and preferred to be a host rather than a guest.

Four o'clock came and went. There was no sound from upstairs, not even a creaking of the bed, so she assumed Jenni was still sleeping, and that reassured her. She so wanted Jenni to get well, for her sake of course, but also so she could see her return to being the lively, happy woman who had marched briskly through her front door the night before. Was it only twenty hours ago? It seemed so much longer.

Then her phone rang, loudly breaking the silence and she fumbled to catch it and stop the noise. It was Isabel at the other end, as she might have expected.

"Hi! Pat called me earlier. My God, tell me what happened? How is Jenni? Can she talk? I'm so sorry you have had the unforeseen bother…"

"It's been no bother at all, but she is still very poorly. She's asleep right now."

"Look, I'll come down to Bristol to fetch her tomorrow. I can borrow a car."

"Oh, no you won't, Bel! The woman stays here until she's completely better. The Pat person, whom you both know, is an excellent doctor. She is a specialist in treating malaria, and she wants Jenni to stay with me. I can look after her without any problems."

"But you sounded like you were really mad with me when you texted back. Like you had some grudge against having her. I wouldn't even have suggested it if I'd thought that."

Jane lowered her voice and almost whispered, just in case she was overheard.

"Oh, that was just me being stupid. You know me and my prejudice about nuns. I expected her to be all religious and try to convert me. She's not like that at all, is she?"

"No," Isabel chuckled. "Not at all! Jane, you can be dense at times."

Jane heard her hesitate, as though she was debating what to say next.

"Why do you think I sent Jenni in your direction, eh? Because I wanted you two to get to know each other. I think you could be good friends, at least. And I know she is seriously independent and thinking of leaving her Order."

"Bel, you are a witch."

"So, you've told me before, on several occasions. But for now, just take care of my friend for me, will you? She's been through a lot, and has had a really tough time in the last few years with all the troubles and violence in Rwanda and the DCR. And malaria is no joke. It might still kill her."

"Don't say that, please!"

"I'm not joking. She's been exposed so many times. But she's been trained never to complain. If she says she feels unwell, then it must be serious. Will you tell her I'll phone again this evening, to see how things are going?"

"Yes, OK. And Bel?"

"Yes?"

"Do you have any wild idea how to make marmalade?"

"Not a clue. What a crazy question! Bye!"

Jane went up the stairs as quietly as she could and peeped her head around the bedroom door. Jenni was curled up like a hedgehog under the duvet and seemed to be asleep, so she tiptoed nearer and then went around the bed to take a look. Isabel's comment about malaria being life-threatening had frightened her so much she wanted to be sure Jenni was still breathing.

Then, as she leaned over her, and lightly touched her forehead to feel how hot she was, the woman's eyes flew open and she looked up like a startled deer waking in a thicket. They both jumped back from each other, and said simultaneously, "Sorry, I didn't…"

Jane got in first. "I just wanted to make sure you were OK, that you weren't burning up. I didn't mean anything."

"No! Sorry. I was asleep. That's why I was startled."

"How are you?"

"Not too bad. But I still ache all over. I think I could do with some more paracetamol."

"I'll get the packet of pills for you."

Jane reached over and produced two tablets of 500 mgs each. She passed Jenni a glass of water and watched as she swallowed them. Then she said, "Isabel called, asking after you. She says she'll try again tomorrow."

"What did you say? I feel so bad I couldn't complete the full assessment like she wanted."

"I said you are unwell, as you are. But I also told her I am looking after you and Dr. Pat is an excellent physician, so she mustn't worry about you. She had some crazy idea about driving down to Bristol to pick you up. But she doesn't even have her own car right now, and knowing Isabel's past history with motorways, you'll be much safer here with me. I'll take you back to London when the time is right."

"You're very kind. I'm sorry to be such a nuisance."

"Will you stop apologising? It's getting to be a bore." Jane heard herself sound really brusque, but it was only because she loved having Jenni here in her bedroom, in her bed for heaven's sake! It may not last for long, this fantasy she was enjoying, but she wanted to sustain it as long as possible.

She ventured to pick up the thermometer and take Jenni's temperature properly once again.

Jenni answered, "Sorry. Oh, sorry for always saying sorry. I will try harder, I promise!"

Jane pretended to ignore her, but was secretly amused. She held the little gun against Jenni's forehead.

"38.5. it's going up higher again."

"It usually is, after a sleep, but I do feel somewhat better, truly, and my headache has eased. The paracetamol will bring it down some more."

"What would you like to do, stay in bed, or come down to watch TV for a while? I can lend you my dressing-gown. Your own pyjamas are in the dryer if you need them."

"Maybe tomorrow I could change back into them. Yours are very comfortable. May I keep them on for the night?"

Jenni then remembered how she was supposed to not act like some female floosy, but as a devout disciple of her order of nuns.

"Jane, could I ask you to fetch me my haversack, please? There is a little black book inside which is my missal and book of daily devotions. It is about the time I should recite the evening office. And also, maybe my knitting, if it's not too much bother."

Jane jumped back two feet and nodded. "Sure thing. I'll fetch them now," and almost bolted from the room. Well, that did the trick.

Jenni reluctantly heaved herself out of bed and held onto various pieces of furniture to make her way unsteadily to the bathroom. She felt like an old lady, and the face she glimpsed in the mirror over the washbasin looked like death warmed up.

"No need to pretend," she thought as she used the toilet. "I need prayer as much as anyone, and no way could anyone see me as a sexual predator in this state! Nothing could be further from reality."

She sat on the toilet but the small amount of wee she produced made her aware of how dehydrated she was, what with the sickness and all the perspiration. So she washed her hands and then drank a couple of glasses of water from the tap, before she staggered back along the landing to bed. Jane was there at the bedroom door to catch her as she almost fell forwards, and she sagged with relief against the strong arms which guided her across the room.

"Come on Sister Jenni," said Jane. "Back into bed with you. I've brought your knitting and your prayer book for you. I'm not sure what your normal position is for prayer, but I guess you can do them lying down in bed, can't you?"

"Yes, smiled Jenni, and in spite of all her resolutions to be cool and distant, and spiritual, she heard herself almost flirting. "I'm often at my best, lying in bed." Which was a completely untested assertion, and outrageous. And had popped up out of her mouth from nowhere.

"I mean," she backtracked hastily," I can pray anywhere, and right now, in bed seems the safest place for me."

"You just take your time," said Jane, coolly. "I'm going to fix us some dinner. How does a chicken fillet and broccoli bake sound?"

"Wonderful," whispered Jenni, "Just wonderful." The idea of fish for fasting on Fridays had floated away, obviously.

"And I bought some crème brulée for dessert."

"Even better."

And Jane left Jenni to her devotions.

Into the Rough

Chapter 14

A Quiet Night In

Jane's typical Friday night routine involved a sweaty hour or two at her local gym, and then a few beers in front of a boxed set of *Law and Order* or some other American cop show on the telly. But tonight, she was cooking, properly...and from scratch, and attempting to produce a light but tasty meal, suitable for a woman who had just nearly been at death's door. She even made a little sauce to put on top of the chicken, and then went upstairs to see how the patient was faring. She'd given Jenni at least an hour to get on with her praying. Surely it couldn't take all evening?

She tapped on her bedroom door, and when she heard a muffled "Yes?" went in to find Jenni propped up in bed gazing into her phone, and looking surprisingly downcast. She had pulled a long and multi-coloured scarf from the knitting bag, but the prayer book lay unopened on the other side of the bed.

"What's the matter?"

"I'm just reading a message from my friend Sophie in Brussels. She says my foster daughter is pining for me, and for our home back near Goma. And I must say it's made me rather homesick for Africa as well. Even having this rotten malaria has reminded me of all the golden years I spent there. Things will never be the same if I can't return. But I know I can't."

Jane realised once more just how little she knew about Jenni's past life and the years she spent teaching in West Africa. But she also saw how a day in bed had made her house guest weary and despondent. She needed a change of scene for a few hours.

"Could you manage to come downstairs for some dinner? Then you could maybe contact your friends again on *Facebook*.

Or perhaps we could watch a film together. An hour or two sitting on the sofa might make you feel better."

"Yes, of course. I don't want you to have to wait on me anymore than you have already."

Jenni swung her legs out of bed, and Jane made her accept the offer of her blue dressing-gown. She wrapped it around herself and Jane thought how slim she was. There was virtually nothing to her. The woman needed feeding up.

She lifted her feet and put them one by one into a pair of her own slippers. They were slim, pretty feet which had obviously never been cramped into tight pointed toes or wrecked by high-heels. Something else about Sister Jenni for Jane to find attractive, damn it!

"Lean on me if you like," she said.

Jenni grabbed her arm as she stood. "The room's spinning a little. Thanks."

Together, they descended the stairs slowly, arm in arm.

Jane settled Jenni on the settee and covered up her legs with a light tartan throw. Then she went into the kitchen and emerged with a tray of hot food which looked equally as edible as the lunchtime fish had been. There was an accompanying glass of sparkling water with a twist of lemon in it, and Jenni sipped from the glass as she waited for Jane to return with her own meal.

They ate together in quiet harmony. Silent meals were a standard tradition for Jenni, and Jane as well, for living alone meant she normally never had company to talk to.

Jenni had made a sign of the cross and whispered a brief benediction over the meal before she ate it. Jane wasn't so surprised by this. It was just a ritual which she assumed was second nature to her visitor, and she supposed she just had to tolerate such little quirks.

In a strange way, Jane's solitary lifestyle where she always had to do everything for herself, and no-one was ever there to make her a comforting cup of cocoa, or bring her breakfast in bed, was probably no less austere than anything the convent life had forced on Jenni.

She thought of this, not with any sense of self-pity, but with a new idea that maybe making some radical lifestyle changes in her own life might be as much a challenge for her as for her visitor. When she met Ms. Right, it might be harder than she expected to adjust. Could she really cope with moving to Australia?

"Do you always say a grace before you eat?" she asked, trying not to appear too nosy, or ignorant about what nuns did and didn't do.

Jenni shook her head. "No, not always. But tonight, why wouldn't I give thanks that I've been sent an angel to cook and care for me? And where did those lovely flowers come from? They look and smell beautiful."

Jane could recognise a touch of the Blarney when she heard it, but she was pleased in spite of herself that Jenni had noticed the flowers and had also enjoyed her food. She turned the words around into a joke on herself to hide her confusion.

"Well, that is something I've never been called! An angel. Do you think there are many atheist angels up above?"

It was out of turn maybe, but she had to be honest with Jenni and let her know she considered the whole flummery of religious practice and belief in something as irrational as Christianity to be simply a delusional waste of time.

Jenni was obviously considering her reply and took some time before she asked lightly, "You're not a believer then?"

"'Fraid not. I'm not one of your religious types. Never have been. Not that I probably wouldn't admire much of what you've done with your life. I'm sure you've helped a lot of people you know, leading a good life, being a nun and all."

Jenni shook her head. She even seemed to find this statement ironically amusing.

"Oh, far from it! Please don't assume anything about the saintliness of religious life by looking to me as an example. I was a very bad nun. And while I may not have broken the letter of the Rule all the time, in spirit I have rebelled and rejected it more than you can ever imagine."

"But you still pray? You said you were going to say the Evening Office earlier."

"Yes, and I tried. Every now and then I try again. But words, words, words – they are just like sawdust. Jane. So if you think I am likely to be shocked by you saying you're an atheist, think again.

"I would love it to be that simple for me. It would be a great relief if I could just say I don't believe in God or anything beyond this world anymore. But it is way more complicated. Every belief about love and redemption I once had has been stripped out from under me and hung out to dry years ago, but I can't quite walk away. Let's just say God and I quarrelled bitterly ages ago and now we simply don't speak to each other anymore."

"But . . .?"

"I go through the motions, that's all. Like a caged tiger, my growl means nothing. I think the behaviours of the Powers-that-be in the Church, the child abuse and all the cover-ups, the corruption, have finally killed my spirit."

Jane rose and collected both hers and Jenni's empty trays. This honesty, and the desolation behind the woman's words set her aback, and she immediately wanted to comfort Jenni, and perversely reassure her that things weren't as bad as she imagined.

But she was a complete novice when it came to anything theological or philosophical. She wouldn't know where to start. All she could do was offer solid, physical comfort, and do Jenni the honour of accepting what she said and not disbelieving her.

"Well, no need to worry about religion anymore tonight. Let's think about the here and now. Remember I said I bought a couple of crèmes brulée earlier?"

"Yes."

"Well, I'm fetching them now, for our dessert. There is some crunchy sugar on top which you are supposed to burn under the grill I think, but shall we bother?"

"No, they sound just fine as they are."

Jenni sounded relieved not to have to talk anymore about her religious beliefs, and Jane decided to keep her distracted, talking about far more worldly matters. They ate their creamy puddings together, and Jane told Jenni about an advert she'd seen on the TV for a little blow-torch you could buy, solely to scorch the topping on crème brulée.

"Can you imagine? Talk about inessential nonsense!"

"I'd need to see it to believe it," said Jenni. "But now then, any more thought to your big marmalade idea? Will you be at home tomorrow? If you are, we could try it together. I hope I'll be feeling better then, and might be able to help."

"If you're on the mend, OK. We can download a recipe."

"On the mend . . . that is an English expression I've never heard."

"It means, well, you're on the mend! Getting back on your feet, you know, bucking up!"

Jenni looked quizzical. "Bucking up? Not bucking off then, like a horse?"

"No! But if I say anything else you don't understand, do ask me."

"I am an English teacher. I should know these idioms. But I have lived in French-speaking countries for so long, one's brain cells drop off, you know?"

"Do you dream in French then?" It was a question Jane often wondered about bi-lingual people.

Jenni thought. "Yes, I do. And in the French dialect from Quebec, my mother tongue, you understand? But when I lived in the Congo for twenty-five years, I started to think and dream in the local African language we spoke there. Maybe one day I will be dreaming in English, if I stay long enough."

"I hope you do...stay I mean," said Jane gruffly. Jenni seemed not to notice, but carried on talking.

"So tomorrow we cook together? That would be nice. And is it possible Dr. Pat might have some empty spare jars at home? She could bring them when she comes to give me the next injection, and then we could fill some pots to sell in aid of GASP."

Jane had never, in her wildest imaginings, thought any marmalade she made would be edible enough to sell. But she remembered a previous Christmas, in 2017, when she had taken her nieces and nephews to see the film Paddington Two.

She recalled there was a big marmalade making section in it, where Paddington and his prison inmate friends had made enough for the whole prison population. She didn't expect Jenni would have seen it, but it was just the right sort of silly film to cheer her up.

"I know a film which might help us," she said. "I don't suppose you watch much Netflix."

"What's Netflix?" said Jenni, answering her question for her.

Jane took that as a big fat 'No'. She easily found the film online, opened it and then sat down next to Jenni on the settee in front of the TV.

Before long, they were both deep into the little drama, and when Isabel phoned Jenni halfway through it, as she'd promised earlier, Jenni said briefly. "Can I call you back Isabel? Sorry, but there's this really exciting film on about a cartoon bear right now, and we are getting to where he's been sent to prison…It's very tense."

Jane could hear Isabel on loudspeaker laughing like a drain, and knew Isabel would make no sense of this. She'd think Jenni was delirious.

"What's the film called?" she heard Isabel persist through the phone.

Jenni turned and asked Jane to remind her of the title.

"Paddington Two."

Jenni relayed the information on to Isabel. "It's called Paddington Too, apparently, like the railway station."

"Oh. Well, call me back when it finishes, darling, and don't worry. I think it has a happy ending."

"Isabel sounded surprised we were watching this film, but I really like it." Jenni snuggled back down under the wrap very close to Jane's side. "I can't remember when I last watched any film."

"Oh? Stick around with me, Sister, and you'll see a few more," said Jane. And she wondered if she should amend her *Her Space* entry form to add 'avid film buff' to her list of hobbies. She had a whole pile of DVDs stacked behind the sofa which could keep them both going all winter. But Jenni was only there for the weekend, or a few days after.

As the marmalade making scenes unfolded, they weren't much use as a training manual for marmalade making for novices, but what *was* as delightful as the film, was the slow but inevitable way Jenni's head dropped sideways onto Jane's shoulder, and then how her warm body eventually snuggled itself up against her. The Canadian fell asleep wrapped close to her like a baby. For a new and delightful way to spend a Friday evening, this wasn't too bad, not too bad at all!

Into the Rough

Chapter 15

Aunt Lucy Would Have Been Proud

Jenni woke with a start when the film finished, and Jane flicked over to the ten o'clock news. She was very worried Jane would think it shocking to have her sprawled all across her on the sofa. She blamed her malaria and the painkillers which were rendering her far sleepier and now more relaxed than usual. She would have apologised, but remembered just in time that Jane had forbidden it.

So, while Jane was in the kitchen washing and putting away the supper dishes, Jenni stood up, stretched and felt she should return to bed. Before doing so, she summoned the energy to return Isabel's call, and to bring her up to speed with the last twenty-four hours.

Isabel sounded very concerned about her health on the phone.

"You poor woman! I know what malaria is like from personal experience, but I have never had the nasty strain which you have."

"Yes, I wasn't a pretty sight this morning, but I am on the mend, as Jane says, and another couple of days and nights with good sleep and the medicine, and I should be back to normal."

"How is my friend Jane behaving?"

"She's very kind. The atmosphere was rather, how you might say, '*un petit froid*' to start with, but she seems to have decided I'm not going to seduce her anymore."

"What on earth do you mean?" asked Isabel.

Jenni told her of her theory about Jane being homophobic, and that her host had probably assumed Jenni must be rampantly gay if she was a friend of Isabel's.

"She's very straitlaced isn't she? But her heart is kind

beneath the fierceness. I am trying not to scare her too much, though I did stupidly fall asleep on top of her earlier, while we watched the little bear film."

Isabel gave a definite shriek of laughter.

"What's so funny, eh?"

"Jenni, my dear, Jane is the most out lesbian in the whole world. Hasn't she shared that with you yet? She hasn't got a bisexual bone in her body, and I can assure you, if you thought she was like Frosty the snowman because she suspected you might be gay, you are way, way off the mark."

"Then what was the problem? Why didn't she like me?"

"She's was probably just frightened of you that's all. She always had been phobic about nuns. And she's such a committed and mouthy non-believer. I'm sorry, I should have warned you. But I almost forgot you are a Catholic nun still. You are so much one of us these days."

Jenni sighed, "You mean, I act like a normal human being some of the time. Huh. Thanks a bunch of bananas."

"Not what I meant darling. You could never be normal. You are far too original and talented. But the main thing is, will you two be all right together from now on? You don't have to pretend with her you know. I thought you might be good company for her, do her some good in fact, and cheer her up. She has been very depressed and down recently. I've been worried about her."

"Yes, I have picked up on that. The house here has no character, as if no-one lives here. But tomorrow we have a joint enterprise. She says we are going to make beaucoup de marmalade."

"Why marmalade? That doesn't sound a very Jane-like thing to do at all. She only has a kitchen because it came with the house."

"Because she bought the marmalade special oranges at the supermarket, and it is January, I think. Isabel, please tell me…why is the film we have just watched called Paddington Too? Who else was supposed to be there as well? I fell asleep in the middle."

"No, darling. I'm sure it was called Paddington TWO. T. W.O. after Paddington One, as in *un, deux, trois*. It was the second film in the series. Not Paddington *aussi*."

"Oh, so that is much simpler than I thought."

"You are silly, to be worried about that or anything else. Just take the medicine and just get better."

Then she added, "But if you want to make marmalade you need to find out if Jane has bought any sugar. It's not a commodity I found very much of in her house when I stayed there. You will need at least a kilo for every kilo of oranges for Seville orange marmalade. They are very bitter. That is something I do know."

"Ah, so life is not so simple after all. Well, I need to go to bed now, lovely Isabel. Jane has given me her bed to sleep in. She is very generous beneath the grumpiness."

"Well, that's certainly more than she did for me when I stayed with her, bless her. You are very privileged. I don't think she can hate you as much as you thought, eh?"

"No, I don't think she hates me right now. At least I hope not."

"Goodnight, Jenni," said Isabel firmly. "Sleep well, and I will call you again tomorrow. I can hear Bryony's key in the door, and she will be coming home exhausted from the late shift at the hospital. I must go."

And she disappeared.

Jane now appeared at Jenni's elbow and grasped it firmly.

"Upstairs with you, now. You need to go back to bed."

"Isabel says we need lots of sugar for marmalade. And, don't worry, I can return to the little gym to sleep tonight. I don't mind."

Jane looked almost angry.

"Certainly not! You are in my bed till you leave. Now come along!"

She almost pushed Jenni up the stairs and into the front bedroom.

Jenni laughed inside to think how her words might be misconstrued. If they were just normal free women who fancied each other, who knows what might have happened. But she was trapped in a loveless marriage with an institution that didn't allow divorce. And Jane? Who on earth could guess what

Jane's situation was? She hadn't even spoken about being gay. Was there anyone special in her life? Any significant other?

Meanwhile Jane continued to supervise her as bossily as the old Mistress of the Postulants had done when she was first admitted into the religious life. She stood close by to make sure she cleaned her teeth and then watched her climb obediently into the double bed. When she lay down, Jenni noticed her pillowcases had been changed yet again to fresh cotton ones and the bed sheets were all smoothed out.

"Where will you sleep?" she asked.

"In my little gym, as you call it. I'll be fine. Don't worry. Now good night, and if you have a relapse and need me in the night, don't hesitate. I shall be cross if you don't wake me."

Bossy or not, Jane was certainly a good carer, and Jenni lay down very peacefully and obediently. Her arms and legs didn't ache quite as much anymore, and she knew her temperature had dropped. She thought she was out of danger and practised the new phrase she'd just picked up again as her eyes closed. Yes, she was definitely 'on the mend'.

Jenni slept late the following morning, and was only just up and dressed when Pat arrived at 8.30, with another doxycycline injection to give her, and a prescription for mefloquine to take her forwards. The doctor had also brought along an old cardboard box of assorted empty jam and chutney jars, which she put on the kitchen table.

"Jane called last night and mentioned you might need these for some reason! I also picked up a couple of kilo bags of sugar for you on the way, as she asked. What on earth are you both up to?"

"Oh, a little seasonal activity, just something to amuse Jenni this morning," said Jane hastily. "Let me pay you for the sugar." And she pressed a couple of pound coins into Pat's hand.

Pat told Jenni to roll up her sleeve and gave her the injection, and then checked her temperature and blood pressure and felt her pulse like doctors did in the old days.

"You'll live," she said, with a twinkle in her eye. "But I don't want to hear any nonsense about you going back to

London yet. If Jane will have you, I think you should rest here for the rest of the week."

"What? I'll go mad! And I'm sorry, I can't take mefloquine. I'm allergic to it. It makes me suicidal."

Jenni didn't want to sound rude, but she couldn't think what she could do in this narrow little townhouse, day after day for a whole week, especially as Jane would be busy at school most of the time.

"I'll prescribe you an alternative drug then. I have some in the car. But Doctor's orders, you must stay put here in Bristol," replied Pat, obviously not caring at all for Jenni's finer feelings, or even sanity.

"I know you have your lap-top with you. So on Monday, you can call Isabel and ask for some very light work to be sent by email. And while you're here I will do the same. There are plenty of things I need your advice about to do with GASP. But I don't want you leaving the house, and certainly not trying to go out in the cold at all or think of going back to London by train."

"I have a half day again next Friday. I can drive Jenni back to London then," chipped in Jane, standing at her elbow.

Jenni met her eye and tried to work out how annoyed she was at the thought of having a lodger for a whole more week. But Jane was her usual brisk, business-like self and seemed unfazed by the idea.

"I thought I was on the mend," Jenni tried arguing. "Couldn't we go tomorrow?"

But the glare she received from both the strong-minded women with her told her there was no chance. She was well and truly grounded.

Marmalade making was quite a palaver as Jane described it, (which was another new word for Jenni.) At this rate, she would be improving her range of English idioms, faster than her knowledge of domestic skills.

They were soon up to their elbows in orange peel and sticky juice. But working side by side, they followed the online recipe to the letter, and within an hour produced between them quite a satisfying amount of bubbling, mixture simmering away in the only really large saucepan which Jane possessed.

"How do we know when it's ready?" Jenni carefully watched the pan to make sure it didn't boil over.

"I'll ring my mother and ask her," said Jane. "She'll know. Hang on."

The conversation sounded very funny, as Jane's mother could not believe her daughter was doing any cooking, let alone making preserves. The phone was on loudspeaker, so Jenni heard both sides.

The second half, after the opening pleasantries, went as follows.

"You are doing what?"

"Marmalade. I'm making marmalade."

"But you normally play golf on a Saturday!"

"Not today. Just tell me how we check when it's ready."

"You need to put a little spoonful on a chilled saucer and leave it in the fridge for a few moments. Then push it with your finger. If it wrinkles, it's done."

"Great. Thanks, must dash. I'll call you later."

"But who's *we*? Who have you got there with you?"

"Oh, no-one to worry about. She's a nun."

"A nun??"

"Yes, a nun. Don't sound so disappointed."

"What are you doing with a marmalade-making nun?"

I'll tell you later. Bye!"

Jenni had already found a saucer and was putting it into the fridge.

"You're missing your golf then. You should have told me," she said.

"Shut up. It's fine. Pass me a spoon, and let's get the jars sterilised in the oven."

"Not bossy, eh?"

"No, just decisive."

Jane picked up a tray of washed jars and slid them into her preheated oven to heat up thoroughly. It was spotless, because she never normally used it. Then she pushed Jenni down onto a chair and handed her a pen and a roll of sticky labels.

"Here, Sister. You can write the labels, with the date. It's a quiet little job and not too heavy. I'm pulling out that saucer from the fridge now, and trying the wrinkle test."

Jenni was highly amused by all this decisiveness. She picked up a pen to start her task, but stood up and watched with interest when Jane spooned a little orange jelly out of the saucepan and put it on the cold saucer. She blew on it slightly, and then offered it to Jenni.

"Why don't you do the honours?"

"What do you mean?"

"Push the marmalade."

Jenni pushed the blob a little with her finger tip.

"Look, it's definitely wrinkling! We should turn off the heat immediately and stop it over-boiling."

"Or boiling over," said Jane.

Ten minutes later they stood together and admired their handiwork. There were eight jars of marmalade standing in a row on the kitchen counter, each with a neat label in Jenni's curly French-Canadian handwriting.

Jane screwed down the tops.

"Finished! Now I am going to make us some toast with the leftover syrup in the base of the saucepan so we can see how the stuff tastes,"

Jenni helped by pulling down two of the plates in the rack and picking up a knife, and the butter dish.

As they sat together and shared the hot buttered toast and marmalade, along with some coffee, Jenni said, "You know, I don't think I have ever enjoyed cooking so much as this. And I have never had home-made marmalade. This is very good."

"No, I haven't either," said Jane. "You know, for two middle-aged women, we are quite ridiculous. We are obviously both novices at the simple joys of domestic life. It's like we've been in the army or something. There is so much to learn. And I only bought those oranges on a whim, because the sign said they wouldn't be available for very long. How crazy was that? I'm sure I would not have done it if you hadn't been here."

"Yeah, so I have spoiled your weekend. You would have played golf if it wasn't for me. I heard your mother say so."

"I can play golf anytime," shrugged Jane, and then she smiled at Jenni and added quietly. "And you haven't spoiled my weekend at all."

"No? Honestly?"

"No. And one thing you should know about me, Sister Jenni, is that I am like George Washington. I cannot tell a lie."

"Don't call me Sister. I know you only do it to tease me."

"Well, that's true. But it suits you and you should let me do it. It means I treat you with respect. Maybe I'll just call you Sis."

"You should respect me anyway because I must be around eight years older than you. Not that I'm counting the years of course."

"If you're fifty, then you still look damn good. Now let's leave the kitchen and come back to the sitting room. I want your advice about something."

Jenni was intrigued and went along with her, happily.

Chapter 16

HER SPACE OR MINE?

It had taken until then for Jane to figure out how she was going to come out to Jenni. Generally, people could tell simply by looking at her. She wasn't sure if Jenni was just so dense that she needed it spelled out for her, or if Isabel had already given her a heads up, and she was far too straight and polite to show she knew.

Anyway, Jane decided to give her a little tutorial, by inviting her to look at the *HER SPACE* website, and ask her to give her some feedback on the next crop of possible matches which would be coming through.

"Come here and sit on the settee. I'll set up my laptop so we can both see the screen."

"What's the site?"

"It's a lesbian dating site."

"Oh and why are you showing it to me?" Jenni's tone was less than positive. "Do you think I'm so sex starved and pathetic I need an online outlet for my romantic yearnings?"

Jane was surprised. This was the sharpest response normally mild-mannered Sister Jenni had ever given her.

"No, I wouldn't presume. Not you! Don't be an idiot. This is for me. I'm the one who applied to them and set this thing up. I'm the one with a sex life so dormant it's under Siberian permafrost."

"Oh, I thought you meant…"

"You thought I was getting at you? Wow, Sis, as if I'd go anywhere near invading your space with inappropriate assumptions! No, I just need your wise advice. I'm looking for a good woman here, and I reckon your taste is better than mine."

Jenni was stunned into silence, but she obviously got the message that Jane was trying to get across. She watched as Jane signed in, and then clicked on the list of possible matches the computer had found for her.

"There are a lot. Has anyone responded to you personally?"

"Yes. In the folder across there, those are the folk who have expressed an interest, who say they'd like to meet me. But I'm too scared. I haven't even posted a photo yet, and I haven't messaged anyone back yet."

"Is this site safe?"

"I reckon so. Do you want to have a look with me?"

"O.K."

Jenni sounded very cautious, and Jane wondered if she'd gone too far, if she'd put her foot in it.

"Nothing might come of it," Jane said quickly, "And if it does, it's mainly about finding new friends."

"Right… just new friends? Not to have sex then?"

Jane felt Jenni's mind begin to run towards the truth, and swallowed nervously. She wished she hadn't started this caper, and even hearing the word *sex*, said with Jenni's husky accent, confirmed that thought. While she dithered and was tempted to abort the whole session, Jenni nudged her in the ribs.

"Well, go on. I'm not going to die of shock looking at a few lesbians, am I?"

"Aren't you?"

"No, of course not. I wasn't born yesterday, even if you seem to think I was. Get on with it. You might find your heart's desire right there in front of you."

"Well, O.K." Jane cautiously pressed the OPEN button on the file, as if it was red-hot.

They looked down the list of hopefuls together. Jane saw members of her own tribe parade in front of her, just as she had before, very friendly, pleasant gay women, forty and over. Most of them had been braver than her and had put up selfies of themselves.

Jane could see they would have made great mates to play a round of golf with, or meet down the pub for a drink, but not one made her knees tremble. The person sitting next to her on her settee, the pretty but androgynous one wearing old jeans and a faded sweatshirt, she was more likely to do that, even though she thankfully seemed oblivious of her charms.

Jenni looked closely at the pictures. "Why not read a few of the messages?" she suggested. "It says here, you been noticed."

"OK."

Jane read a note from a nice looking woman who was wearing a polo shirt in a picture obviously taken the previous summer, unless she lived in Queensland or somewhere south of the equator. Her face was very tanned.

"Hi, you sound just my type. How about we get to know each other better, and then see if we're a matched pair? Send a photo honey. Don't be shy."

"Honey? She's American. I don't think so."

"Don't be so racist! What's wrong with the Yanks? They can't help it. You should respond."

"I wouldn't know what to say. And I don't have a photo."

"Well give me your phone and I'll take one. We can soon sort you out."

"Jenni, no!"

"Come on. You've paid good money for this. You need to make it worthwhile. Give me your phone."

Jane sat there and wondered how things could have got so far out of hand. She had just wanted Jenni to know she was gay, not have her houseguest start acting like some marriage broker. But Jenni seemed unstoppable.

"Hand it over! Now!" she urged.

"Oh, very well..."

And in the end Jane let Jenni take several pictures of her, full face, and profile and then standing by the window to catch the light through the glass.

She had to admit they weren't too bad, they flattered her in fact. When she reviewed them, she seemed to be looking quite sexy as she smirked at the camera in a couple of shots, especially after Jenni had pulled faces at her and made her want to laugh. She decided to have her own back and said, "Right, now your turn, Madame. Stand by the window like you made me do, and give me a smile."

Jenni gave a shrug which was positively Gallic, but she complied, and when Jane had snapped several, and then looked back at them, her heart gave a positive flip. Now if a photo of Jenni had appeared on the website, she'd have been online in a flash!

Jenni was as self-deprecating as usual. She peered over Jane's shoulder.

"God, I look awful, like death warmed up. Erase them, won't you?"

"I certainly will not!"

"Well you will have to save them as a 'before' in a 'before and after' set of shots. When I get better from this nasty bug, you can take my picture again, and then hopefully you'll see a difference. But back to your task. You should respond to a few of these women and upload your picture so you can send them a jpeg. There are at least seven messages in your in-box. Go on! I am going upstairs for a lie-down, so you can work in peace."

Jenni was walking towards the door, and Jane said, "Yes, I'm sorry, you must be exhausted. But where's this new bossiness come from, eh? You're not my school principal you know."

"No, but if you tell me what to do for my health, then I can do the same for you. I'll be fine. Do you want me to mark your efforts when I come back down?"

"Do you think I should?"

"Yes. I don't want you heading off the fairway with any unsuitable types."

"Golfing allusions now…what next?"

"Oh I can talk about it some, just not play it."

"One day I'll teach you."

"You reckon? That would be nice. But I'm expecting you to have eloped with one of those lovelies by the time I move to Bristol, if I ever do."

And Jane was left alone with her gallery of potential girlfriends. Well that was a lively little spat! Jenni certainly had spirit, and a sense of humour. Jane could easily see how she would learn to enjoy arguing with her.

With Jenni gone, her enthusiasm for the online search waned, but she did as she'd been told and scrolled through all the messages and looked at the assorted faces. Three or four looked honest, decent people, and so she wrote back to them and attached her photo, but she realised she was steering well clear of any who seemed to live in the southwest of England.

This was a signal she didn't want to rush into meeting anybody, not even to play golf. She put the shortlist replies all into the draft box, and then did something which pleased her more. She transferred and saved all the pictures she'd taken of Jenni into a folder on her phone, and named the folder *Paddington.* Cunning, eh? Looking at the Canadian's face gave her instant pleasure. Oh dear...

Jane turned on the television quietly and flicked to Sky Sports, which was covering a test match in Sri Lanka. She put her feet up on the settee, and decided to enjoy the cricket for the rest of the morning.

Into the Rough

Chapter 17

Perfectly Honest Reasons

Jenni had left Jane alone downstairs for perfectly honest reasons. She was indeed tired after all the activity, and her headache and other aches and pains were returning. She went to Jane's pleasant bedroom, and fell back onto the bed fully clothed.

But there were deeper feelings banging away in her brain, and she needed some solitude to bring them under control. There were two people in the house right now; one of them she thought she understood, but the other woman bewildered and frustrated the hell out of her.

Jane, big, bossy, beautiful, Jane, was pretty much an open book. She hadn't been kidding when she had said she couldn't tell a lie. If Jenni spent any more time with her she was pretty sure she could get to the bottom of what made her tick, why she seemed so depressed. But the other one? Well, she was a piece of work. Jenni mistrusted herself, big time, and she despised the cowardly, frightened actress she had become.

She knew what game she was playing. She was really good at concealing her true feelings in plain sight, hiding behind her metaphorical habit, putting out the 'friend to all the world' assurance of someone who lived apart from, and above, the rest of messy humanity.

The school principal, the dedicated missionary, the person who disdained to have any personal possessions beyond what she needed to do her work...these were all masks she wore. Thirty long years living as a nun had taught her so well. But she wasn't fooled.

Watching Jane nervously tremble as she'd opened that dating website, and then looking alongside her at the dozens of brave, and emotionally vulnerable gay women who were honest enough to say they were seeking partners, had done something profound. It had convinced Jenni of her own emotional bankruptcy. She had been a coward at eighteen, when she had first applied to join a nunnery, and she was still a coward today.

It had all been a sham, boldly encouraging Jane to be brave and follow up her possible contacts. Who did she think she was kidding? Jenni knew she herself was as gay, or gayer, than any of the women on that screen, and probably even more than the sporty woman in whose house she was staying.

But instead of being honest, and simply saying to Jane, "I know you wouldn't look at me twice, but I really fancy you and I wish you would take this fifty-year-old virgin to bed and show her what sex is," she just knew she didn't have the courage or self-confidence to take the risk, and probably never would.

She now understood why her God had walked away from her in disgust. She was just a hollow shell of a woman, all form and no function anymore.

Jenni tried to find any redeeming features in herself, and just couldn't. Tears began to roll down her face and she buried her face in the pillow and started to cry, as silently as she could, but as openly and as vulnerably as a baby.

She wasn't used to crying. Nuns didn't cry, did they? They were trained to maintain a zen-like calm under all pressures, and she had rarely cried since she was a child. Then her mother's illness and early death from breast cancer, and her father's subsequent descent into drunken rages and sporadic violence towards her and her brother, had certainly made her cry. She had also cried when her first and only real love had run away from her in high school.

But those tears had been shed a long, long time ago. There were a lot stored up inside her, and now the flood gates opened. Jenni cried for the long-lost, pretty young thing she had once been, for all the love she might have had in her life, a life she had chosen not to lead.

The weakness caused by her malaria, and by the side-effects of the antibiotic she was on, broke down all the walls she had lived behind for her entire adult life, and she knew, somehow more than ever before, that there was no point in trying to rebuild them again.

Downstairs, Jane soon tired of watching the cricket, which was proceeding at a snail's pace, and then just as it was picking up pace, the umpire declared a break for tea and refreshments. Even in Sri Lanka, it seemed the old British traditions of cricket teas were sacrosanct. She turned off the TV and then gave herself a better treat, looking again at the photos of Jenni on her phone. Nice. Perfectly lovely.

She was filled with a simple desire to look after this woman, to give her love and care, and everything she needed to be the sweet, rather magical person she was. Jane had never met anyone quite like her. She knew her head was being turned, but just couldn't resist much longer. Her first idea of booting Jenni out of the door as quickly as possible seemed to have disappeared. Now she wanted to capture her and hold her close for ever.

Then she thought she could hear something, a distant mewing sort of sound. She wondered if a neighbour's cat was crying at the window outside. But as her ears adjusted, she realised with horror, that the sound was coming from upstairs, and it was of a woman crying. It was Jenni!

Without any hesitation whatsoever, Jane hurled herself up the stairs and threw open her bedroom door. Of course she should have respected her guest's privacy and not invaded her space. But Jane didn't act like that when she was in full impulse. She didn't have the nickname Buzz Lightyear among her colleagues at school for nothing.

"Jenni! Darling! What's the matter?"

(Well, if Isabel could call Jenni 'Darling', why couldn't she?)

She ran across to the bed, and tugged Jenni up into her arms, rocking her like a baby, and tried to console her.

"Sshh, Sshh. What's the matter? What's upset you?"

Jenni just sobbed into Jane's shoulder even harder.

Jane remembered how she herself had cried at Isabel's wedding, how the tears had simply poured out of her against her will. This bout of uncontrollable weeping from Jenni, though, seemed even more passionate and heartfelt. Jenni clung to her, as if she were a sturdy tree in a howling hurricane, and seemingly could do nothing but sob into her shirt.

Jane just held her, and rocked her, back and forth, until eventually Jenni was all cried out. She shuddered against Jane's firm, fit torso, and let Jane rub her back and the tense muscles in her neck and shoulders.

"I'm sorry. I'm so, so sorry," she whispered.

"Hey! Remember what I told you about all that apologising? Never, ever say you're sorry to me again. You don't need to, and I don't want to hear it, OK?"

She hugged Jenni fiercely. It seemed the most comforting thing she could do, and thankfully Jenni wasn't complaining. They stayed like that for several minutes.

When she thought it safe, with one hand, Jane pulled out some tissues from the box on the bedside table and passed them over. Jenni took them, and wiped her eyes.

"I guess that was something you needed to do," Jane said, trying not to pry.

"Uhuh."

"Not a symptom of malaria, then? Or caused by the prospect of being holed up with me for a week, I hope?"

"No."

Jenni mopped the worst of her tears up and dabbed her swollen eyes. She added, "But some malaria tablets do drive you crazy. Lariam, for example, which Pat first wanted to give me, can give you suicidal tendencies. I was quite reassured when I first found that fact out. It stopped me following through with it once, when I was prescribed tablets in Goma. They sent me crazy."

"God, you're not going to want to top yourself now, are you?" said Jane, with such an expression of horror on her face that she made Jenni give a little laugh.

"No, I'm off Lariam for good. You don't need to put me on suicide watch."

"So?"

Jane did need some answer, so she could understand and help. "I'm normally hopeless with feelings, with being empathetic, I mean. I'm very dense. Anyone who knows me will tell you. You'll have to help me out here."

Jenni looked up into her face and said, "I will explain everything to you, one day. But it is a long, long story. I'm afraid you are dealing with a real mess of a person here, Jane, I can't lie to you. And all I can plead is please forgive and accept me for what I am. I'm just like an ostrich chick emerging through a very hard and thick eggshell, and I'm not in control of my own emotions right now. Will you believe me when I say I haven't cried like this since I was eighteen?"

"Yes, I do. And whatever you say or do, or how you want to behave, that's OK with me. You may have noticed I have a hockey player's broad shoulders. I can cope. You don't have to be stoical and brave with me if you don't feel it. Now go and wash your face and then let's go downstairs. I need you to check over my answers to the ladies on the *Her Space* website, before we have some lunch."

Jenni gave a wan smile, and let Jane release her from the hug. As she watched her go through to the bathroom to repair her ravaged face, Jane had a thought and joked,

"Hey I can guess what made you cry! Did you look at all those pictures of women and realise what you've been missing, down there in the jungle all these years?"

Jenni just turned on the wash-basin taps and said nothing in reply. Jane bit her lip and cursed. Maybe she had touched a raw nerve after all? But then, maybe she was the obtuse one here? If Jenni could look at pictures of gay women and feel regret, was it so impossible that one day she might look at Jane in the same way, and feel something for her?

If there was even the faintest chance of wooing Jenni into her heart and into her bed, nun or not, Jane knew she would work to keep that chance alive. Whatever demons or dragons Jenni was running from, the love of a good lesbian was surely the way to rescue her, and Jane was more than happy to be her knight in shining armour.

Into the Rough

Chapter 18

Never Eaten Haggis?

When they met again in the kitchen, Jane presented Jenni with a steaming bowl of Heinz tomato soup and a large chunk of wholemeal bread. It looked good, and its unique taste was even better.

"Here, have a knob of butter in the soup. It will make it even richer, and you need some flesh on those bones. I think you must have lost five pounds in the two days you've been here!" Jane cut off a slither of butter and floated it on Jenni's soup.

Jenni smiled her thanks.

"I shouldn't have butter. But I do love the taste of it. It is one thing you never see in West Africa. Is it just two days since I came? I can't believe it. I feel I've known you for ages, and your place already seems like home."

"I know. Weird, isn't it? And we've had a month's worth of trauma already. You have turned my world upside down, do you know that, Sis? But I'll tell you something, for nothing. Before you came, I was in a worse place than you say you are. I was so depressed I couldn't feel a thing. It was like I was outside the human race. But now, whatever's ahead of us, I feel I'm connected back in again."

"That's great, but I can't see how I can take any credit. I've been nothing but trouble for you."

Jane shook her head.

"That's not true, as you know very well." She gave Jenni another little glare. "I want to be your friend. Will you let me?"

Jenni stopped lifting the spoon which was halfway up to her mouth, and felt a spark of human warmth rise up from her middle. It was just like the TV advert for this tomato soup, and it made her smile spontaneously.

"Your friend? Even though you don't know me, and you hate nuns?"

"Yes. I'm sure you can bring me around if you try. I may hate nuns in general, not knowing any of course, but I don't hate you. I think you are warm and funny, and French, and a ragamuffin, and we have loads in common. And I have this uncontrollable urge to sort you out, get you some decent clothes, and take care of you."

Jenni's heart flew around like an out-of-control drone. This was as close to a declaration of love as she had ever heard, and it was honest as well. She swallowed the hovering spoonful of soup, and then said, "Jane Walkley, it would be a privilege to be your friend. I would be honoured."

But then she frowned in mock annoyance. "But what is so wrong with my clothes, hey?"

"You dress like a tramp. Don't you have anything else to wear but torn jeans, an old flannel shirt and a faded sweatshirt?"

Jenni laughed as she finished her soup and chewed on the bread like a homeless person in a soup kitchen.

"You know, actually I don't. I do have a credit card I can use, and I intended to go clothes shopping when I first came to London, but I have never had the time. I did buy some stout boots, but what you have seen of my couture is more or less it. It all fits in my backpack. But hey, I am respectable! I have three pairs of panties and two bras. I also have a spare pair of socks."

"What did you wear in Africa then? When you were Principal of a big girls' school for God's sake? Don't Africans like their officials to dress smartly?"

Jenni gave a little shrug. "Yes. I had three blue dresses. And I wore sandals. It was always hot. Occasionally I did wear the little veil which our order still produces for high days and holidays, to show respect, and when the Bishop came to visit. But I left that in Canada."

"Well, I think we can do better than that. My wardrobe is packed with clothes I never use, and you can take your pick, even though most of them will swamp you. But we are more or less the same height, and it looks like we might be the same shoe size. You will definitely need more warm clothing, and some brighter colours. You'll never get through winter in London without a padded jacket and some lined trousers."

"I'm knitting myself a scarf," said Jenni, stoutly.

"I saw, and while you are with me, you can finish it. I love it. But let's get you a slightly wider range of outfits, eh? There's a sale on at Rohan right now, and we can choose some extra things online. I have an account with them."

"I can pay."

"I know, with your credit card! But this is my house and my treat, so let me have some fun, why don't you? Let me do something nice for you."

Jenni dropped her eyes, and hid how delighted she was to be spoiled like this. It was such an unusual feeling, to receive, instead of give. She was a professional giver, she realised, and it was time to receive instead. Like divine grace was supposed to be, Jane's generous offer was unforced, and seemingly without any strings attached.

"Thank you. That would be lovely," she murmured.

"Good," said Jane. "Let's get on to it straightaway! Now there is something else I want to run by you. How strong do you feel? Might you be up to coming out around the corner with me for an hour or two tonight?"

Jenni's ears pricked up. Going out, hadn't that been a prohibited activity only a few hours earlier, when Jane and Pat had both told her she was confined to barracks? She nodded. "Yes, if you are with me, I would like to go somewhere, for a little while tonight."

Jane smiled, with a look of relief on her face, and explained further.

"You see, contrary to the impression I might have given you, I do have a few friends in this world, and I forgot before, but I've been invited to celebrate Burns night with some mates from school. It's just a small party, but it's a little tradition we have, and it's at someone's house not far from here, a short walking distance in fact."

"Burns Night? I don't understand. What is that?"

"Burns night. It's an old Scottish tradition, in memory of an

18th century poet, Robert Burns. We sit around and drink Scotch. Then we all eat haggis and recite his verses, and tell jokes."

"So Jane, are you Scottish?"

"Heck no, but I drink Scotch, and when I'm sufficiently tanked, I can tell very funny jokes."

"And what is haggis?"

"Good question. I think I'll leave you to find that one out. Now let's go upstairs and choose you some suitable clothes to wear for the party."

"Won't your friends be surprised to see me?"

"Astonished. Yes. They think I'm the nun around here. But they will love you. I'm only taking you to show off that I do have a wonderful friend."

"Now you are being the silly one. But Jane, can I beg one favour of you?"

"What?"

"Don't introduce me as a nun, eh? Let's just keep that to ourselves, please?"

"Sure. No probs," said Jane, but Jenni could see the request puzzled her a little, as it had herself. She just wanted to shrug the 'religious' tag off her shoulders, and be accepted for who she was, a penniless waif and stray of a woman, finding a new way to be herself in the world.

Upstairs in Jane's bedroom, Jenni watched as the fitted wardrobe units were flung open and dozens of hardly worn, good quality tops and trousers, jackets and giléts were revealed. There wasn't a skirt among them. The only problem was that most of them were for a tall size fourteen, and her scrawny body was barely a ten. But Jane seemed confident there would be something for her.

"We only need find you something for this evening, and then we can buy you a nice selection in your own size online. Here, try this shirt, and these black pants. They are a twelve. I think I bought them when I was on a diet and had big ambitions about losing weight."

Jane obviously expected her to strip off in front of her, and Jenni suddenly felt shy and self-conscious. She said as much.

"Shy? Don't you remember yesterday morning, I had to toss you, mother-naked, into the bath-tub? Come on sweetie, you can keep your bra on. You're quite safe with me."

Jenni laughed and nodded, and started to pull off her clothes. She was being ridiculous. Jane, sporty, PE teacher Jane, would be a veteran of the women's locker room, where she imagined girls strolled in and out of the shower naked on a regular basis. But suddenly, Jenni wanted to be attractive for this woman, not the undernourished, fever-wracked bag of bones she knew she was right now. It wasn't simply modesty which made her hesitate. It was old fashioned body shame.

Jane reassured her though, by briskly ignoring the hollows in her neck and shoulders and passing her over a bright white shirt to wear and a pair of stretch black pants which didn't hang too loosely on her. Then she pulled out and gave her a lovely warm cashmere sweater in a bright scarlet, and finally a cute tartan waistcoat, which had adjustable straps. Jane pulled them tightly so the garment no longer seemed in danger of falling off her shoulders, and then turned her around to show her how she looked in the wardrobe mirror.

"There, doesn't that cheer you up? I'm certainly no fashion plate, God knows, but I tend to buy quality. Red really suits you. These are all yours from now on, and I can throw in a whole packet of new black tights which will keep your legs warm through the nasty weather to come."

It was like Christmas. Jenni was delighted with the novelty of wearing quality, virtually new, clothes, which hadn't come from the cheapest store she could find. Jane found her several more new items of clothing and insisted she took them.

Then they spent the afternoon window shopping online, in the sale at Jane's favourite outdoor clothes outlet. *Rohan* apparently created good quality clothes for travellers and sportspeople, which were guaranteed to be made ethically and with the highest standards of protection. Jenni was quietly happy they weren't buying throw-away junk clothes.

She baulked at the prices though, which were high, even in the sale, but Jane put her hand over hers and said fiercely, "Sshh, My treat. Just shut up and choose exactly what you like and think you'll want to wear. You will be stuck with these clothes for a while, because Rohan gear never wears out. That's why shopping from them is a good decision."

So Jenni chose, even adding a long padded duvet coat in a bright red colour to top off her other selections.

"My little backpack won't hold any of this stuff," she protested, as Jane was about to finish the order, and Jane countered that argument by simply adding a large, scientifically designed, lightweight rucksack to the list.

"Sorted. It will all be here by Thursday. Now, what would you like to do before we go out this evening? Do you need to sleep, as you obviously didn't get much chance earlier?"

"Can I borrow your Wi Fi connection and try to talk to my girls in Brussels? I would like to *Facetime* them if I may, from my lap-top."

"Certainly! Why didn't you ask before?"

Jane watched as Jenni subsequently enjoyed a long and obviously loving conversation, first with her elderly friend Sophie, but then with the two young African girls in her charge. They were chattering away in French, and then in an African language, and then in English once more, as Jenni wanted to hear from Patience, who had been abducted from Nigeria and so didn't speak French, how she was settling into their Belgium school.

Jane could hear how well Jenni interacted with the youngsters, and what a kind caring teacher she obviously was. However badly Jenni thought of herself...however harshly she seemed to be judging herself, Jane could clearly see she was an exceptionally good and kind person, and fiercely intelligent.

"My friend Jenni," she said to herself, and it felt good. Even if nothing more was possible, even if she could never chase away Jenni's fierce dragons and rescue her, have her for herself, being her friend would still be a very joyful, positive thing.

And she was very, very grateful to Isabel for having the low guile and cunning to arrange for them to get together. The woman was a witch, but a good witch, and she was right when she said she knew just what Jane needed. She needed someone just like Jenni!

When they set out a few hours later, Jenni relied on Jane to help her navigate the network of suburban roads through her estate. She'd been wrapped up warmly in one of her host's duvet coats, which was all enveloping and far warmer than her own leather flying jacket. Hat, gloves and her own black leather boots completed the insulation against the cold night, and Jane tucked her arm underneath hers for the short walk.

It took less than five minutes walking in the cold night air before they were at the party. Jenni was welcomed into a bright room, not dissimilar to Jane's living room, but crammed with people already obviously enjoying a drink or three. They were indeed astonished to see her, just as Jane had warned her, but the crush of happy faces seemed very welcoming. Jane introduced her as "My Canadian friend, Jenni," and steered her through the crowds towards a spare seat or two across the room.

"What are you drinking?" bellowed some big guy from the bar area.

"Scotch for me," answered Jane and Jenni asked for a Coke, adding by way of apology and explanation. "Cranky liver, not allowed to drink alcohol."

They managed to hand their outdoor clothes over to a pair of willing hands and then wedged themselves into a sofa in the corner. Jenni's experience of British domestic life was limited to Alana and Stephanie's hospitality, for the first night she had arrived from Canada, and then the few weeks she'd spent at Frank and Trixie's family home.

This was different again, seeing a bunch of adults who all knew each other well, joking and chatting together, and she enjoyed simply sitting quietly and taking in all the various conversations around her. The Bristol dialect had a pleasant inflection, and a tendency to add a double –L at the end of words ending in a vowel, which the linguist in her found rather fascinating.

Dishes of potato crisps and little cheese biscuits were circulated, and then after an hour or so, a large plate of steaming vegetables and what looked like some oatmeal pudding was thrust in front of her with a fork.

"Here you arell," said the man hosting the party. "Get stuck into that, my lovell!"

"What's this?" she whispered to Jane.

"Sheep's offal and blood pudding cooked with oatmeal. Good thing you're not a vegetarian isn't it? But try some. It tastes good, and isn't as heavy as it looks. Scottish national dish. Haggis."

"And the orange veg? Squash?"

"No, swede, or what the Scots call "neeps"."

Jenni tasted it and then said, "Oh, we call it rutabaga in Canada."

She was used to eating anything, including fried termites in Africa, so in principle Haggis held little fear for her. But being only too aware of her delicate stomach, she proceeded carefully, checking every minute or so to make sure it was still in its rightful place.

Jane meanwhile wolfed everything on her plate down like a hungry horse. "Would you like to finish mine as well?" Jenni asked her. "It would be a shame to waste it." And the plates were quickly swapped.

It was a happy, unforced evening where Jane looked more at ease than at any time since Jenni had met her, and it made her happy to see that her friend did have some good neighbours who would be there for her in an emergency, and who obviously knew her well. There was the reciting of various poems by Robert Burns, and Jenni recognised one from her university days. "My love is like a red, red rose that's newly sprung in June..." Poor Burns, he died in his thirties, up in Scotland, which was somewhere else Jenni had never visited, and hoped to see one day.

Towards the end of the evening, when the crowd was thinning slightly, a woman came over and introduced herself.

"Hi, I'm Judith and my husband there by the door is Phil. We both teach with Jane at Reedbridge, and it's lovely to see her bring someone along to these get-togethers."

Jenni returned her smile and said, "It's great to be here, but I'm afraid I won't be staying after this week. I'm just in Bristol on business. Jane and I have only just met. But we've made good friends with each other."

"Well I hope you come again, and stay longer next time. She obviously likes you!"

Jenni wondered what Judith meant, but let it go. Jane caught her eye and came back to get her.

"I can see you drooping. Let's go. I'll fetch the coats from the bedroom." Jenni exchanged another pleasantly bland smile with Judith, and let her drift back to her husband.

The walk home seemed longer than their earlier stroll, and Jenni realised by the time they reached Jane's front door that she was still weak with the malaria. No way could she have been ready to leave on Sunday.

Jane was pretty tanked up on whiskey, but she helped Jenni upstairs as gently as a professional caregiver, and virtually put her to bed. She had Jenni's own pyjamas ready for her, the cosy brushed cotton ones, and when she had undressed and put them on, Jane tucked her in and then squeezed her hand.

"I hope the party wasn't too much for you. It was selfish of me to drag you along, I know, but I don't get out that much and I didn't want to leave you in alone on your own."

"I enjoyed every minute," replied Jenni. "And orange marmalade and Haggis on the same day? My culinary tastes are widening by the hour! Thank you for a lovely time. And for everything. I'm sorry I'm a nun…"

This made Jane laugh.

"Don't be. I've forgiven you already."

Jenni very, very badly at that moment, wanted to draw Jane in for a kiss. But shyness and reserve won the day, as usual, and she just let her squeeze her hand and then quietly withdraw. Learning to be her friend was enough to cope with, for now, and it had been a very long day. By the time she heard Jane gently shut the door, Jenni was already falling asleep.

Into the Rough

Chapter 19

Birds on the Water

The intensity of their first forty-eight hours together surprised both Jane and Jenni, and by Sunday morning it was almost as if without openly discussing it, they jointly decided to calm everything down and simply learn quietly how to get along together. Jenni still felt weak, a shadow of her normal dynamic self, and so was happy to lie-in until nine and snooze, while Jane went out running for forty five minutes on her normal daily circuit. This took her five miles, out to edges of the city and back again. Jenni then heard her return, thump up the stairs, and then dive into the shower.

When they met in the kitchen later, Jane was wearing a tracksuit over a warm thermal top, and looked the picture of health. She'd picked up the Sunday papers on her route home and passed them over to Jenni. Jenni found the serious British newspapers fascinating, and she was soon ensconced on the settee, with sections of the papers and their supplements all over her.

Jane made a big pot of coffee and a pile of toast and marmalade which she put down in front of her on the coffee table.

"There you go. Get that down yourself," she commanded, rather like an army cook. She passed Jenni a coffee and said, "You do look better today. Less washed out. That's good. I'm pleased the party last night didn't cause a relapse."

Jenni asked, "No, it didn't. I slept solidly through the night for ten hours, which is remarkable for me." Then she changed the subject. "So what else would you normally do on a Sunday morning? I don't want to disrupt your normal routine."

"A pile of laundry, maybe clean the car. A round of golf

possibly. And sometimes I go off into the country. Would you like to drive out for a while this afternoon? You'll be here alone all week, I'm afraid, after today. But we could take a trip somewhere today to show you around the surrounding counties."

Jenni didn't answer, but she looked interested, which Jane interpreted as a "Yes."

"O.K. Let's do that. Will you not go to Mass today, as you're officially sick? I don't think I want you sitting in a cold church somewhere, even if I knew where the nearest Catholic one might be."

Jenni was touched by Jane even thinking about her religious well-being. She smiled and shook her head. "No, there's no secret religious police out there, checking up on me. Would you believe me when I say I haven't attended Mass once since I left Canada? Like I said, I am a very bad nun. Going to Mass makes my heart physically hurt these days. It upsets me so."

Jane looked alarmed. "Oh, well then, I won't bring it up again. But if you did want to go, you only have to say the word."

"No, I don't. But I would like to take a drive with you this afternoon. That would be a treat."

"Right you are. Then we'll have a snack at noon and then head out while there are still a few hours of daylight. I hate these short winter days, don't you? Bring on the summer!"

Jenni buried herself in the newspapers. There were pages devoted to the new virus which was obviously more serious than the Chinese had originally let on, and cases were springing up around East Asia. But she enjoyed reading the news, and even found some articles about Africa, buried in the inside pages.

Meanwhile Jane vigorously washed and polished her car, and then fixed them both omelettes for lunch, cheese for her and mushrooms for Jenni, as she had said she couldn't tolerate too much dairy. Afterwards, she made sure Jenni was warmly dressed and then pushed her into the front of her RAV4. She pulled out the seat-belt which had fallen to the floor behind the passenger seat as it was so rarely needed.

"Buckle up. It's the law, don't forget."

"Sure."

And they set off.

Jane took Jenni on a pleasant two-hour circuit of the countryside south of the city of Bristol, into Somerset as far as the village of Chew Magna and the flooded valleys of the Chew Lakes. The wide-open stretches of water were home to migrating wildfowl and when they parked up, she handed Jenni her binoculars "Here, tell me what you can see."

"I'm not too familiar with European birds," said Jenni.

Jane's clear love of teaching kicked in, and she gave her a beginner's guide to bird watching. Jane was good. She seemed to know the names of everything they saw.

"It's only January. If we were able to come here in March or April, you'd see far more activity on the water. But I also need to take you north of Bristol to the nature reserve at Slimbridge on the River Severn. There are large flocks of swans and geese there right now, having migrated down from above the Arctic Circle for the winter, and that is a sight to behold."

Jenni realised that bird watching was a real interest for Jane. She wasn't totally obsessed with sport to the exclusion of all other interests.

"Yes, I'd like that. I want to learn more about British nature, especially if I move here."

"And will you? Settle here, do you think?"

Jenni felt the warmth in the question, and the slight tremor in Jane's voice, but she wasn't sure how to interpret it. She turned to face Jane, and said, honestly. "Yes I would like to 'settle' in England very much. It's a nice word. But someone will have to give me a permanent job, or I need to find someone to offer to marry me. I know how tough your immigration rules are. Sadly, unlike the birds, I can't simply migrate across continents and settle where I fancy." She had made a little joke of it, the marrying part.

"Which would you prefer then?" Jane laughed. "A permanent job or an offer of marriage?"

Jenni replied very quickly, "That would depend on who

asked me! I think Isabel might give me a permanent job. But for the other…who knows?" Then she looked sideways at Jane and was delighted to see she was blushing. It was just the reaction she had dared to hope for. Who would have thought it? Maybe this attraction she felt wasn't quite as one-sided as she'd imagined.

They soon turned the car for home, and Jane bustled her back inside. "Now make yourself comfortable, and we'll eat something, and then let's watch another film tonight. I have a hundred DVDs and I bet you haven't seen any of them."

"You're right there," agreed Jenni, "so we can watch whatever you like, anything you can bear to see again."

Resistant as she had been to the idea at first, Jenni found the week she spent convalescing in Jane's townhouse strangely restorative. It was good to be still, and secure, after all the moving and crossing of continents she'd done in the last four months.

Every evening she was able to chat to her girls in Brussels, as Sophie lent them access to her own tablet, and Jenni could also monitor their progress and help them with their homework. Sophie was looking after them so well, that she hoped there might be a longer term solution to their welfare and they might be able to stay with the elderly teacher in Belgium on a permanent basis. But it was ultimately down to the police and the social services in Belgium. Sophie worked for the Migrancy Council however, so she was well placed to lobby on their behalf. Jenni guessed she'd never be allowed to bring them to the UK.

Jane came back and forth each day from school and whirled in and out of the house like a spinning top, but she had attached a chart of her weekly schedule on the fridge, so Jenni knew exactly where she was, and what time to expect her home. Jane had gone shopping early on Monday morning, so Jenni started to prepare their evening meals from the ample pile of provisions, and enjoyed having a kitchen to herself. She discovered the joy of cooking and took simple pleasure when Jane tasted her casserole or stir-fry and said, "Hey, this is good! You can come again and be my cook anytime!"

The quiet days spent alone also gave her the opportunity to write a really sensible report for the Righteous Anger Board about the pros and cons of linking up with GASP, and she also brought all of Stephanie's outstanding reports up to date. Even though she was working remotely, she could still earn her place at RA. Doctor Pat, as well, popped in most days to check on her, with work she needed advice about, or issues she needed to discuss.

Above all, spending the week in Bristol really calmed Jenni's spirit. She had never lived in a little house like Jane's, and never before had a domestic situation, with only one housemate. Her childhood home had always been busy, as she was one of several cousins raised under the matriarchal regime of her grandmother.

Then in her community in West Africa there were never less than twenty assorted people sitting down to every meal. Her personal bedroom had been constantly bombarded with staff coming in and out and needing her attention. Even the washrooms, showers and toilets had been communal. The chance of a quiet soak in a deep, warm bath behind a locked door was an unheard of luxury.

From Tuesday onwards, she felt well enough to take short walks around the block, and began to get a feel for the quiet suburban estate. Many of the houses were bigger than Jane's, but it had a safe, family centred feeling, with tidy gardens and things growing up walls and trellises.

Jenni still missed the exuberant fertility of her African home. Everything here seemed very tame and restricted, but she could see how people cared for their tiny plots, and even in the depth of winter there were a few bulbs showing through the bare soil. Jane's own front garden, though, consisted of twelve square feet of grass, period.

"If I lived here, I'd plant a veg patch," thought Jenni, and in her imagination, she could already see an array of beans and salad crops. She hadn't even explored behind the house, which only had access through the back door, as the line of houses were in a terrace. But when she opened the door she looked out onto a pleasant little patio area, with a BBQ and a series of low walls going up the steep bank above. Again, one could grow things up there. She wondered what things grew well in the Bristol area. Oh well, it was a nice fantasy, but it wasn't her house, nor her garden.

On Thursday, as promised, a parcels service delivered a bumper consignment of very exciting looking packages for her. She waited for Jane to come home so they could open them together. She was too excited to do it alone.

When she came through the door about seven o'clock, Jane laughed at her for waiting, but fetched her scissors and then handed them to Jenni.

"Go on then. Let's see what you've got!" Then she watched as Jenni opened all the bags and boxes and pulled out her new wardrobe.

"Oh, wow, this is all too much. But isn't it great?"

She could feel Jane looking at her, as she unpacked everything, and then automatically started to fold up the bags and papers neatly and methodically, to save them.

"You should try all the clothes on, just to check they fit," said Jane. "We can send anything back which you don't like, as well."

Jenni piled up her new clothes and the big new rucksack and staggered upstairs with them. She laid everything out on Jane's bed, and then began to try the various outfits on. Jane appeared at the bedroom door shortly afterwards, and asked, "Do you mind if I come in and watch?"

Well, Jane had bought them all, so even though Jenni did feel as shy as she had before, about stripping in front of her, she nodded. Jane sat down in her bedroom armchair by the window and happily supervised the whole dress-show.

Without a word being spoken, they both knew that Jane enjoyed seeing Jenni getting into her new clothes, and getting out of them, but this didn't have to be a big deal. It just was what it was. Finally, Jenni put on a last pair of the Rohan stretch pants, a base layer and then a pretty turquoise coloured fleece.

Jenni did a pirouette in front of the mirror. "I think I like this the best. I love the colour."

"You're right. It suits you. Everything else fits OK?"

"Yes, I love everything. I'm cross with you for insisting on paying for it all. The rucksack alone must have cost £80. But I am truly grateful. Even after I stopped wearing the convent uniform, I've never dared buy anything like these things. It's like being de-mobbed from the army straight into a high-end fashion store."

"Well, embrace it, honey. You deserve a little spoiling, and it won't do your overdeveloped sense of low self-worth any harm to have a kick up the rear. None of these items is frivolous, or anything more than you will need to survive the British winter."

Jenni realised how right Jane was about her tendency to cling to the 'poverty' idea of her vocation. She could spend money on other people, but never on herself. It was almost as suffocating a rule as the 'chastity' command had been. She had already escaped from the 'obedience' but the other two vows were much harder to shake off.

Jane sat back in her chair like a fashion editor directing a shoot, and then beckoned Jenni over, saying, with a nod of her head. "Come here and let me take the label off the back of your trousers."

Jenni went across the room, and then was taken by surprise as Jane deftly pulled her down onto her lap.

"Oy!"

"Sit still. I'll undo this string. It's still attached to your waistband."

Jenni realised she's been tricked into sitting right on top of Jane, whose look was positively wicked. Well, two could play at that game. Their faces were so close, she could almost feel Jane's breath against her ear, so she put her hands up on either side of her face and did what she had secretly fantasized about doing for the last five days. She boldly kissed Jane full on the mouth, and then even added her tongue to the exercise for good measure.

"Everything has strings attached," she whispered, after her little attack. "If you buy me all these things then you have to put up with being thanked for them."

"Eek!" was an approximation of the squeak which came out of Jane, as she was obviously shocked by Jenni bouncing her into a French kiss, but the surprise didn't seem to be a nasty one.

Jenni felt herself being pulled down towards Jane's chest, and then her kiss was returned with a passion which was both very scary and exhilarating. Jane held her tight, and seemed quite prepared to keep kissing her, both on her mouth, and then along the line of her chin as far as the edge of her ear.

But the suddenness and the force of their connection seemed to stun them both, and they broke apart quickly. Jane's blue eyes were almost purple in the evening lamplight, and her blonde hair stuck straight up from her forehead. She looked delighted, but disbelieving.

"What was all that about? I thought I was the cheeky one. And you're asking me to believe you've never done this before?" she asked.

"Never," gasped Jenni. "Well at least, not for so long, I've completely forgotten what it feels like."

"Well, in that case, oh my," said Jane, using one of her mother's old expressions. "My, oh my, oh my!"

Chapter 20

A Week is a Long Time in Politics...And in Other Things as Well...

Jenni tried to stand up, to escape from whatever it was which had just exploded between them, but Jane held her down, firmly, to carry on sitting across her knees. The warmth of the woman, the sheer physicality of having someone to hug and to hold, was so exquisitely affirming that she wasn't going to give it up very easily.

"Answers, please. I thought I was the 'only gay in the village' here."

She knew the jokey allusion would be lost on Jenni, but she'd made her point. She continued. "'Fess up! That sort of kiss doesn't come from nowhere."

Jenni's face had turned from its normal faded tan to a delicious pink, and Jane was impish enough to enjoy seeing her so far out of her comfort zone. It meant she might get some honest answers out of her.

Jenni looked intently at her fingernails and kept her eyes down. But when she spoke, Jane knew she was telling the truth.

"It just felt the right thing to do. Um... if you want to know, I've fancied you since I first landed on your doorstep, and you stood there, so cross, and so cold, and so in charge of yourself. Of course I hoped you might be gay, but I didn't dare trust my instincts until Isabel put me right and you pushed the lesbian website in front of me. It takes one to know one, doesn't it? But with me, you've had to deal with someone like those old Egyptian mummies, all wrapped up and embalmed. Pretty dead inside, but disguised by a lot of tightly wrapped bandages. It has taken me all week to have the courage to tell you how I felt."

Jane smiled, but kept a tight hold around Jenni's waist and

shook her head.

"You are far too fanciful with your language, you know. But I agree, you're certainly a dark horse, Sister Jenni Argent, like the Lloyds Bank advert. You come across as so cool and charming, such a balanced, disciplined, gentle person. And you've suffered this nasty malaria so gracefully. I know you haven't felt at all well. I told myself all I wanted to do was look after you, and make you decide I wasn't such a bad person after all. But I lied. Of course I fancied you, like mad as well. Who wouldn't? You are flipping gorgeous."

"And a middle-aged, about to be de-frocked, nun, who has as much sexual experience as a sixteen year old."

"I'd like to de-frock you anytime. Bring it on!"

Jenni almost choked with laughter. "Jane, that's really vulgar."

"Yep. But there's no point lying. So, you know how dense I am. Can I take it you're really and truly gay, no kidding?"

"What do you think? Yes, I'm gay. I like women. I really like you. I've fallen for you harder than any woman I've ever known. But even though I've known hundreds, and lived with dozens of them all my life, I've never slept with any, or made love."

"Wow! Then it's real. It's not just my fevered imagination. We've both confessed it, and I for one, feel as happy as a pig in muck about it."

"Jane! Your use of similes gets worse by the minute," said Jenni, but she was smiling. "My problem is that, like I've never played golf, I've truly never actually had sex. Kissing you just now, was the boldest thing I have ever done. Isn't that ludicrous?"

Jane looked at the woman nestling on her knee. So she really was virgin territory? Wow. Jane wouldn't really count herself any great expert at sex. She wasn't in the same league as the virtuoso Isabel, who in her twenties, had cut through pretty young girls like butter, even tutored many of them. She'd also broken quite a few hearts, and Jane had been kept busy, consoling all the Exes. But she'd had the obligatory few short-term liaisons at university, and there was one girlfriend before

Felicity who had hung around for a term or two.

There had been nothing like this attraction she felt for Jenni though. No-one had come close, and Jenni's whole reaction to sex, positive or negative, would now come down to how well Jane treated her. It was a huge responsibility.

"I'm a PE teacher, not a grammar buff. But I know what I'm good at, and that's teaching. I will have the greatest pleasure in teaching you some sex ed., if you'll let me. And with me at least, you know I'll never be shocked. You can tell me anything, ask anything, and we can take our time. We can try anything. And it won't go any further. It will only just be us. Feel free to go with your instincts. This is a doctrine free zone."

"I was brought up with the demands of the confessional. I have the most boring tendency to keep picking over my sins and analysing them."

Jane had a moment of insight and said, "But I would bet a thousand pounds, you've never confessed to any priest about the biggest issue in your life, your sexuality. Am I right?"

Touché! Jenni looked up, straight into Jane's clear, honest blue eyes, and nodded her head. "Yes. Mea Culpa. You are quite right."

"Well then. This is just between us then. But I am now officially absolving you from that, and from all other past sins and misdemeanours. You've suffered way more than enough."

"I can't be let off that easily. I need some penance. I am a natural masochist. You should know that by now."

"Then let me kiss you again, and I'll forgive you anything."

Jane lifted her arms from their position around Jenni's waist, and gently pulled her back towards her. Then, almost reverently, she opened her lips and claimed Jenni's mouth for a long, heart-stopping kiss. It was even better than the first time. The woman's kiss was like champagne. Jane felt as giddy as a teenager.

When they stopped, Jenni put her head down on Jane's shoulder, and just like the time when she had burst into floods of tears on the previous Saturday morning, she let Jane wrap her up with love, to be hugged and rocked in a way no-one had done for her since she'd lost her mother.

Jane was physically very instinctive, and simply held her close. She was loving this just as much as Jenni, but she was also processing what they should do next, how they should deal with this new open attraction between them.

After a while, Jenni lifted her head and raised her eyebrows in a silent question. She'd obviously been thinking in the same direction.

Jane said, "I have to take you back to London tomorrow. How are we going to handle that? I would have left it until Sunday, but I have an inter-school hockey tournament to run all weekend."

"I don't know. It will be hard. But nothing about this is very straightforward."

"What do you mean? Basically I think it's pretty simple."

"Yes, I am sure you would think that, but what if we progress to having sex, then I am absolutely a bag of nerves about what you will think of me, how you might react when you see me…"

"I've already seen all of you, don't forget, and I like everything about you."

"But I'm sure I'm frigid sexually, that I couldn't climax, and I would barely know how to give you an orgasm. I'm even getting to the age when the menopause will soon kick in."

Jane looked exasperated.

"Woman, you worry far too much! I'll be your personal trainer and show you how to have sex, if you honestly need lessons. It is a course I'll be delighted to take you through, step by tiny step. And whether or not you think you can, I'll show you how to come to an orgasm. Very few women have a physical reason not to, not unless they've been savagely cut, as in FGM. Follow my lead darling. It's not rocket science."

"But I am weighed down with so much baggage. Psychological baggage. I'm a bundle of neuroses."

"Oh, Jenni, do shut up. Look, forget all the voices inside your head, telling you you're unworthy, or not up to being my lover. I'm more concerned about how we deal with the hundred and twenty miles which will soon be between us, and the demands of our current jobs. Somehow, you just have to persuade Isabel and Pat that your rightful place is down here in

Bristol. Can you do that?"

"Your...your lover? What a beautiful, and frightening word."

Jenni was obviously still processing that mind-blowing idea, and hardly listening to Jane's more practical concerns.

"Yes, of course. What else would you call it? I'm not messing about here. I'm forty-two and damn tired of being celibate. I want you to be my lover. I want you in my bed as often as possible. What else did you think would happen next?"

"Oh, oh, I hadn't even got that far..."

"But how does the idea sound to you? If this is just a little experiment to you..."

Jane tried hard not to feel a wave of disappointment sweep over her.

"Oh, no, of course not. I only... Jane, no-one has ever wanted to be my lover before, or maybe it was me, never letting anyone get close enough to ask the question. But yes, the idea sounds just so wonderful! I can't take it in!"

"It's not such a terrible word, is it, 'Lover'?"

"No, it's a perfect word. Please Jane, if you really think you might cope with me, deal with all the baggage I bring with me, then yes I would be honoured to be your lover, just as I want you to be mine."

"Great," said Jane. "Then we easily can work out everything else. Trust me. Let's pack your clothes away, and then let's go down for supper. I can smell something very tasty coming from the kitchen." She released Jenni, and eased her off her lap. "What have you been cooking for us today?"

"Korean spicy pork and Asian vegetables with noodles. I just saw what you bought on Monday, and took the recipe from the internet. I've never cooked anything like that before, but it seems OK."

Jane said, "Glory Be! It's like I've died and gone to heaven."

Jenni turned and looked troubled for a moment, still seeking reassurance. "You know I still feel what I'm doing is wrong. That I have no right to feel this happy. I've been so indoctrinated that part of me still feels God condemns me, even though I know it's not true. Heaven seems very far away from where I might end up."

Jane tossed her head, and then said something which for her was completely out of character.

"You do talk tosh at times. Have you never considered that God might have had a hand in this? That He or She has set this whole darned thing up? Bringing us into each other's lives? Making this happen?"

"God...or how about Isabel?" laughed Jenni.

"Well Isabel may have had a hand in it as well. But who put the idea in her head? Maybe we have to trust in the ultimate goodness of the universe. Perhaps that's why this has happened. So who are we to argue?"

"So what are you saying, you old atheist? That God might even exist after all?"

"I'm not saying that. I wouldn't presume. But doesn't it say in the Bible, "God is Love."? Why don't we just leave it there for now?"

Jane pushed Jenni towards the stairs. "Come on, let's go downstairs and eat. I'm starving." And they went to enjoy Jenni's new recipe together.

Chapter 21

Virgin Territory

Jane couldn't repress a grin as she watched her new lover serve up the delicious looking food. Not bad for just a week. Not bad at all. But Jenni had just mentioned Isabel, and despite what she had said, Jane had a crazy idea she should be phoning Isabel and asking for permission to date her Canadian friend.

Isabel had always been gently condescending towards her about her lack of success with finding the right person, and had openly criticised her choices. Of course she'd been right before, especially over Felicity, but Jane couldn't bear the thought of her criticising this new relationship with Jenni.

But again, if she didn't disapprove but encourage them, then Isabel would be impossibly self-satisfied that her idea of playing Cupid had worked so quickly. No, let her guess the outcome of the proposed visit for a while longer. Jane wanted Jenni just to herself, and didn't want anyone, even Isabel, interfering.

As they washed the supper dishes together, Jane realised she'd bagged herself a real extra to the Jenni package – the woman was a natural chef!

Jane glanced at Jenni as they retired to the living room. It was clear that her new girl-friend was becoming more nervous by the minute. As the time grew closer to bed-time, Jenni began to look as nervous as the girls at school did when they were waiting to sit a piano exam. She even started to pace up and down and kept glancing at her watch.

In the end Jane couldn't put up with it any longer and said, "Oh, for God's sake stop fretting, darling! I'm on my period. That's why I was so cranky last week. PMT. You won't be able to get inside my knickers, or do anything like 'that' tonight, so sit down here on the sofa with me and calm down."

Jenni's relief was palpable. She sat down next to Jane, and took her hand. "Oh, thank you. I'm such a fool, and so ignorant about how I could make love to you so I'd make you happy. I feel I should get a book out of the library first, you know, to do some prep..."

Jane grabbed her around the neck and pretended to throttle her.

"What am I going to do with you?"

Then she pulled her over and looked into Jenni's deep grey eyes.

"You know you have ridiculously long lashes. They really shouldn't be allowed."

Jenni wanted to look away, but Jane held her gaze without blinking.

"I'll tell you what I would simply like us to do tonight. May I ask you one little favour?"

"Hmm?" Jenni felt as though she was a mouse in front of a cat. But Jane's eyes were kind and a deep blue, and her face, with its short tousled crop of blond hair, was warm and promising, not threatening, ...well, almost not...

"May I come back into my own bed for our last night together?"

"Last night?"

Now it was Jenni who felt stricken.

"Last night of this, our first week together, silly."

"Oh."

"I just want to hold you, and cuddle you, and kiss you a bit. Would that be acceptable?"

Honestly, thought Jenni, Jane was a consummate flirt. And for someone who was such a natural butch, she sure knew how to beguile and creep up on one.

"Just cuddle, and kiss a bit?"

"Hmm-hmm."

"I think I could manage that..." Jenni broke into a broad grin.

"Good. Then let's go to bed. I'm knackered."

Then Jane pulled Jenni up the stairs so fast her feet hardly touched the stair-carpet.

They both put on their pyjamas like teenage girls on a sleepover, and then, after teeth cleaning and pill taking etc., they climbed into bed. Jenni laughed as they both tried to get in the same side.

"You choose," she said. "It's your bed."

"I normally sleep on my left side, because I busted my right ribs playing hockey a few years back, and they're still slightly painful."

"We have so much to learn about each other. I have a scar on my arm where a guy with a machete decided to have a go at me."

"Show me!"

"Oh, it's faded now. It was a long time ago."

"Show me!"

Jenni began to roll up her sleeve. The long scar was indeed so faint now; she almost forgot it was there.

"I can't see properly. Take off your jacket."

Jenni slipped out of her pyjama jacket and stood there by the bed, half naked. She suddenly had the strongest feeling of heat between her legs and sexual longing for the woman who turned her to the light and grabbed her forearm.

"Where?"

"There, running down the line of the bone, from my elbow to just above the wrist."

"Oh, my God, that's terrible. You could have been killed."

"But I wasn't, unlike some of the people I was with. It was in Rwanda, Jane, many years ago."

"Oh, Jenni…"

Jane bent down and gently kissed the scar, and then the crook of her elbow, and then her shoulder, and then her breasts.

Jenni's heart leaped up almost to her throat, and she gasped, "Take me into bed, Jane, now. Please make love to me…"

Jane picked her up bodily, as if she was lighter than a child, and tossed her down on the mattress. Left side, or right side ceased to matter, as Jane pulled the duvet over them both, reached out with her hand to kill the light, and then proceeded to console Jenni for every wound, every pain, every little ache she had ever received.

It was the very best feeling in the world. The night was still young, but it matured considerably as midnight approached, and when Jenni's temperature rose, it wasn't caused by the malaria.

As the clock struck twelve, Jenni, finally, at the ripe old age of fifty, learned just how wonderful sex could be. Jane's love-making wasn't at all as she'd imagined it might be, not hard, rough, and bordering on the aggressive.

Instead, Jane's touch was unbelievably soft and gentle, almost tickling to start with, interspersed with feathery kisses which sent shivers all over her body. She began to drop warm kisses, like little gifts across Jenni's neck and then down the sides of her breasts.

Jenni felt her nipples spring to attention, and grow unbearably tender as the blood rushed to them and they began to swell of their own accord. Jane's lips began to play with them, licking and kissing each in turn until Jenni writhed in pleasure under her. She felt a burning heat curl right down the centre of her body from her breasts down to her crotch, and she decided she wanted more sensation, not less. This was pure joy, and she was greedy for more.

"Please!" She grabbed one of Jane's hands and pulled it down inside her pyjama bottoms, opening her legs a little to capture it.

Jane chuckled, and instead took Jenni's warm cotton pyjamas trousers, and pushed them right down to her knees, from where Jenni kicked them off. This allowed Jane to give her what she wanted...the sweetest, most beguiling caresses with her fingers around her light mound of pubic hair and then inside her.

Jenni had never been penetrated by anything other than tampons, and she could feel Jane being extra gentle and cautious. Sensitive she certainly was, but she had a burning need for more touch, more stroking, more of everything. She started to buck against Jane's hand, stroking herself against the fingers, and then felt a warm flood of sexual fluid come from inside her vagina and toss them both on a tide of sexual arousal.

"Wow, you're here for me already, Baby," said Jane, her

voice still muffled by her mouth, still busy against Jenni's breast, and then she did just what Jenni hoped, stroke by stroke, faster and faster, right up and over the barricades, into her first orgasm.

It happened so fast Jenni hardly knew what had happened, until afterwards. She realised she had been moaning and panting, and was now coming back down to earth with a glorious feeling of relaxation.

"Hey!" Jenni smiled broadly at her body's own cleverness. "I came. I came! And in less than five minutes! I'm not frigid after all! C'est magnifique!"

Jane raised herself up on an elbow and gave the little toss of her head Jenni loved.

"So we're already in a time-trial race are we? Nice to see you're so proud of yourself, Madame! I suppose my skills as a lover had nothing to do with it then?"

"Totalement, tes baisers sont les plus doux du monde. Je les aime...Jenni realised her language of love was in French, but Jane seemed to be getting the gist of what she was saying.

She believed Jane when she said she was on her period, so she just kissed and caressed her from the waist up, and didn't try any return serves, but she was already fantasising about what she could do when Jane might be match-ready. In the meantime Jane continued to be a wonderful lover for much of the night, and took every one of her senses on a magical mystery tour. Their pyjamas at some point left the bed, and they lay together, their bodies touching at every possible point.

Jenni had never, ever, fully understood the power of physical love in the way she did that night. The reality was so much more cherishing, and life-giving than any of her fantasies could have conjured for her.

"Some week!" was the last thing she said as they finally fell asleep, wrapped all around each other.

"Yeah," murmured Jane, her lips hot against Jenni's breast. "Some week."

Into the Rough

Chapter 22

London Calling

The three hour drive back to the northeast side of London the following afternoon gave Jane and Jenni the chance to have a long chat about themselves and what had happened between them. They talked about a host of things, filling in some details about each of their lives, and sharing past histories. There was so much to share, they could only skim the surface, but it enabled them to feel easier and more familiar with each other.

They were in love, but they were still virtual strangers.

"I have so much to learn about you," sighed Jenni, who was very much aware of how little she knew or understood about Jane. Unlike Isabel who had been Jane's best friend from childhood, she knew nothing of Jane's family background or history.

"So, what do you make of me so far?" challenged Jane, keeping her eye on the road. She was more nervous of Jenni's answer than she admitted.

"I can tell you are an excellent driver. And just as I trust you behind the wheel, I know I can trust you to drive our relationship, with firmness and speed and skill, looking ahead to the future, rather than back.

"Next to you, I feel safe, and very happy to be your passenger. It's a relief not to have so much responsibility on my shoulders. Running a large girls' high school with a thousand pupils, year after year in a warzone wasn't exactly easy, especially through times of unrest and violent social collapse. I think I am only now realising how close I came to burn-out. Even if I didn't have the malaria problem, I can admit now that I think they were right to tell me to leave."

"Do you want to share the driving?" asked Jane after an hour or so. "I can put you on the insurance if you like, for the future."

Jenni confessed, "I can't drive, as I joined the convent at eighteen, and anyway my Dad was usually too inebriated most of the time to be a good teacher. Then during all the years I worked in Africa, there were always drivers in the Community's employment who badly needed the job. They would be waiting all day to take me wherever I wanted to go."

"Wow. Then you must learn, ASAP."

Jenni nodded, and said, "Yeah, I'm embarrassed about my lack of a driving license. I feel it infantilises me somehow. It's OK in London, with good public transport, but I can see if I live down here I will need to be able to drive."

Jenni knew it was a priority that she should find some lessons, learn to drive on the left especially, and pass a driving test. How she would ever afford a car was another issue!

One thing they did settle on, as they drove along the M4 to the capital city, was that for now, they were going to keep their relationship private, something just between them.

"Would you mind?" asked Jane. "It's just that Isabel thinks she has to know every last thing about me. And also that she has the right to tell me what to do! I guess we've done it to each other over the years. But I don't want her to put you off me, or have a go at me for invading the sanctity of your vows."

"And you think she might try to do that?"

"She isn't a CEO for nothing, she's very directive, and I know she thinks you're a treasure. If she believes I am lusting after you, she may not let you come down to Bristol so easily. She's always known I was a godless heathen, and she may just assume I'm playing devil's advocate with you, and getting you to renounce your calling."

Jenni said, "Now I think you are the one to worry too much! But, sure, I agree. Let this be our secret. No-one else needs to know yet. We don't even know quite how it will work out, do we? I also think our 'thing', or whatever we call it is too precious to become the subject of office gossip and speculation, however friendly or well-meaning it might be."

Jenni knew exactly what Jane meant about trying to keep it

confidential for a little while at least, though she wondered how long they could keep up the pretence of not caring for one another. They were still exploring what their relationship was; let alone where it was going. Each might have secret hopes, but Jenni certainly knew she had a long way to go before she could think further than the end of the next week, let alone anything permanent. It wasn't that she didn't already adore Jane. She just didn't have the self-confidence to take the lead, or even invent a future for them both.

Jane loved her, she had certainly made that clear, and for some reason she found her scrawny body attractive, but Jenni knew Jane had been badly let down in love before. She was wise to be cautious. In her shoes, Jenni would be as well. But as for her, she was like a teenage boy with a crush. She wanted to be with Jane, to tag along behind her, to spend as much time with her as possible, and to have lots more of the lovely physical education Jane was so good at providing!

They drew near to London, and the traffic began to build. To get to Stoke Newington, Jane went the long way around the M25 and then cut back down into East London. Their last ten miles driving through the narrow streets, and around all the one-way schemes, took almost as long as the first hundred miles had.

"Now, whatever else you do this week, do try and convince Isabel she needs you in Bristol. Let's get that sorted. They've already said they want you to take over running GASP, if the charities merge, don't they?" asked Jane finally, as they drew up outside Trixie's place.

"Yes. Do you think Isabel isn't going to suspect that there's something going on between us?"

"Yes, as long as I avoid being in the same room as her. Isabel can read me like a book, but I think I can keep up a little pretense if we are just on the phone with each other. You have a much better chance of keeping up the pretense, if as you say, you've been trained by the Jesuits. Wasn't it true they never cracked under interrogation?"

"I'm a practised liar, if that's what you mean," sighed Jenni. "But that was mainly to myself. This thing between us, it's so precious to me, I'll do anything to protect it. But I must come back to see you again next weekend. It will be hard enough waiting that long. I'll have to find an explanation to Trixie and the others why I need to come down to Bristol again so soon."

"Tell them I'm going to teach you to play golf. That's true, because I will."

Jenni decided to blurt out what else had been on her mind.

"And to drive. Maybe you can start me off with some lessons. I have to do it, even though everyone drives on the left here. It's scary enough being a pedestrian trying to cross the road."

"Hey, then we have the perfect little cover story. You come down to me on Friday evenings and until we can relocate you, you can get an early train each Monday morning. Lots of people commute to London from Bristol. They'll hardly know you've disappeared."

"I'm sure Trixie and Francis will be happy to have their house to themselves over the weekend, but what about the cost? Won't the tickets be very dear at the peak times on the trains, leaving London on a Friday and getting the morning express back on a Monday morning?"

"Between us, it won't be a problem. What do I have to spend my salary on otherwise? I paid off my mortgage on the house years ago. You must never be anxious about money again, Jenni, love. And you're entitled to spend your salary how you like, even if that old Canadian convent is funding it. I bet they have millions stacked away."

Jenni cast her mind over the rolling acres, and the huge building complex of the convent in Quebec, erected in the 19th century when so many wealthy Catholics built up its endowments. Yes, it was true, her order of nuns probably had more capital assets, and gilt-edged stocks in the bank than they knew what to do with. It was one of many reasons she had become so disillusioned with them.

"I feel sad that we can't kiss each other goodbye, like I want to," she said sadly. "But do come in with me and meet the family. It will look odd if you don't."

"OK, sure. I'll bring your new rucksack, if you take the

haversack and the marmalade."

Neither of them needed to worry about being outed as a couple, because Trixie and her children were simply delighted to have Jenni back, and Trixie, who knew all about malaria from her Sierra Leone childhood, was just full of anxious questions and concern for her health.

"You must have been through it. You've lost so much weight in one week."

"I know, but I'll put a few pounds back on again soon, don't worry."

"Isabel says to only go back to work, if you feel you can, and to work half days all next week."

They welcomed Jane like a good friend and offered her tea, which she accepted. She said to Trixie, "Just make sure Jenni rests over the weekend. I would have liked her to stay down in Bristol longer, but she was keen to get back to you."

"And you have a hockey tournament to organise, don't forget." Jenni spoke cheerfully, to endorse the fact that they had become friends, but their relationship was perfectly sensible and rational. She kept up this front for the next half hour, until Jane bade them all goodbye and reluctantly went down the steps to retrieve her car.

In front of Trixie and the kids, Jenni decided to act like any normal Frenchwoman might and said, "Au revoir, ma Cherie," and kissed her warmly on both cheeks. Jane gave her a very intense look, and half whispered. "I'll call later." And then they parted.

It took three hours or more for Jane to reach home and by then the late January evening fog was swirling up from the River Avon as she turned into her driveway and parked the car. She dreaded going in and finding the house empty and Jenniless, but when she closed the door behind her and looked around her sitting room, she saw a little parcel wrapped up on the settee.

She went across and picked it up. It was light and soft, and she immediately tore off the paper. Inside was the multi-coloured scarf Jenni had been knitting all week. It was now long and a riot of colours, with a fringe at both ends. She shook it out, and then read the note slipped inside with it. "A poor exchange for all your generosity, but every stitch comes with my love. You make my heart sing. Keep warm on the hockey field."

Jane felt tears come to her eyes. It was such a perfect gift. Beautiful, unique and useful. She wrapped it around and around her neck and then felt for her phone. Suddenly the house felt a home once more, and in seven days Jenni would return.

She pressed her number and then said, "Hi…yes, home safely, and I am wearing your present. I love it, and I love you, wonderful lady. Now tell me what you've been doing since I left you in London…"

She sat down on the settee, and started to gossip to her secret girlfriend, her significant other, the person who might well turn out to be her one true love.

Chapter 23

Marmalade and Meetings

By the end of a noisy weekend in the Nabieu household, Jenni was more than ready to return to work, and didn't want to obey Isabel's instructions about working half days. There was no need anymore. She was over the malaria, and determined not to let it attack her again. It was true that the longer she stayed away from malarial regions, the less likelihood she had of falling sick again, and she had no desire anymore to return to Africa. It would be just too far from Jane, who was now the focus of her heart. She was sure she could manage the programmes for RA remotely, as *Skype* and *Zoom* meetings were so much easier these days.

So on Monday morning, she caught the bus with Trixie all the way through the north east of London to the RA office, and was greeted like a returning hero, complete with a haversack full of presents for everyone. Isabel looked at her with a keen, bright look of enquiry, and Jenni did worry for a few minutes that she would give herself away by turning bright red if Isabel so much as mentioned Jane's name. But her naturally sallow skin and faded tan saved her blushes.

Isabel did ask later, "So, how was it, at Jane's? She's a dear person, but staying there for three weeks nearly killed me last September. She seems to use it mainly as a storage unit for all her sports equipment. Did she make you sleep in the room where she keeps her treadmill?"

"At first," Jenni said, and then pushed the conversation sideways. "But it was Jane who made me better. She's very organised and efficient, isn't she?"

"You could say that, except when it comes down to her heart! How did the marmalade making go by the way?"

At this, Jenni was very relieved to be able to change the narrative from Jane's heart, and produced out of her haversack five good-sized jars of marmalade, which she passed around the office.

"There you are, my friends. Some January presents for you." She gave one to Isabel, and the others to Festus, Caroline and Rupert. Trixie had already had hers back at the house, and Steph was out at a meeting at Save the Children's huge headquarters, so she left hers on her desk.

Festus looked very happy. "It's just what my mother used to call, 'Bottled sunshine.' Thank you, Jenni."

Isabel looked in astonishment at her little gift. "So it wasn't just an idle fantasy? Are you telling me, Jane Walkley made this? In her own kitchen?"

Jenni looked blankly at her.

"Sure."

"Why? Has she had a major breakdown?"

"No. She just thought it would be a good thing to do, you know, a little project for a grey January day."

Isabel shook her head. "Maybe my friend Jane is finally cracking up. I have never known her cook anything more than a boiled egg. I bet you lived on fish and chips from the local chippy all the time you were there, didn't you?"

Jenni felt defensive and slightly hurt on Jane's behalf, but she didn't want to arouse Isabel's suspicions any further, and let it go.

"Anyway, please come over to my desk, Jen," said Isabel. "I've been having an initial read of your excellent report on GASP, but I'd like to discuss it with you in more depth."

Jenni and her boss spent an hour talking about GASP, and how it might fit into their profile. Isabel then called Festus over to join them, as she was concerned about the financial implications.

"We could manage it," he said, "as long as Jenni's religious order continues to fund her post, but we'd still have to lose the Bristol finance officer and bring all the accounts to my desk here in London. That way, our whole outfit would break even on the core costs, and we can widen our supporter base considerably."

Jenni was very sad to hear that the young man in Bristol might lose his post. He was only part-time, but she had liked him and thought him very efficient.

"We'd have to offer him redundancy," said Isabel, "And I don't like the idea of leaving Lynne, the admin assistant down in Bristol, there in the office on her own. I would suggest we brought the whole charity's administration up to London, except we don't have the office space here either."

"Don't forget," said Jenni, trying not to sound desperate, "Most of GASP's supporter base live within twenty miles from Bristol. It is very much a local initiative, originally founded by Pat and her friends at Bristol University. I did think, if I was based down there, as their stand-in manager, then I could travel around the local support groups in Gloucestershire and Somerset, and widen the membership. They do need a new leader there. Pat is wonderful, but as the Chair of the Board, she can't permanently spend so many hours in the office as she currently has to."

"Yes, I have thought about sending you down again to the West Country," said Isabel. "But I wouldn't expect you to have to stay with Jane again. We'll make sure you have somewhere much more suitable to live, if the plan goes ahead."

"When do you think you'll make the decision?"

"We have a Board meeting scheduled for next Thursday evening. Can you come along, Jenni, and put the case for the merger? Then, if it's agreed in principle, we might get it in place quite soon. There would be a large communication campaign needed to sell it to both our supporters and *GASP*'s. Oh, I do hate that name! I think it will have to go."

Jenni remembered an idea she'd had coming on the bus to work.

"All the schools they support in Africa are out in the rural villages and communities, aren't they? It's part of the charity's mission?"

"Yes?"

"So why don't we suggest they change their name to *GRASP, - Girls' Rural African Schools Project.* It has a much stronger, more dynamic feel to it. You know, like grasping opportunities. I'm sure the English speaking African partners would go for that. And I can conjure up a French equivalent, if you give me a few minutes to think it through."

"Jenni, that's brilliant. Let's send an email to everyone who is a stake holder and tell them of the plans so far, including the idea of a slight name change. I'll go and brief Caroline about it, and we can include it our next newsletter. Oh, and Jenni, we need a photo of you to go in the newsletter, along with a hundred words or so, introducing yourself. Do you have any pictures? If not, Caroline will take one."

Jenni thought of the photos Jane had taken of her in the Bristol house, but she wasn't going to remind Isabel of her stay there any more than necessary.

"I'll ask Caroline," she said. And they all returned to their respective corners of the room.

One thing weighed heavily on Jenni's mind after the meeting, which otherwise had been very positive for her hopes and dreams. Obviously Isabel and Festus were depending on her continued membership of her religious community, to fund the expansion and her role within it. But they didn't fully understand the spiritual crisis she was enduring.

If she was true to her heart, Jenni knew staying as a nun in the long term would be impossible. She truly wanted a clean break and an honest resignation from the Order. This was quite separate from the other dream she had. If she was free, she could perhaps build a future as a laywoman, with Jane as her life-partner.

Her conscience wouldn't allow her to take money under false pretenses, but how could she raise the same amount herself? Even if she slashed her costs down to a minimum, the overhead costs, of paying national insurance and the other overheads attached to a staff post would be far more than she could earn otherwise.

Jane had said she didn't need to worry about money. But of course she did. Life in England was almost as expensive as in Canada, and she would need to earn her keep, and secure the future for the girls in Brussels. It was a very knotty problem, but maybe, for now, one she could set aside for later.

Stephanie was very happy to see the marmalade when she

returned to the office after lunch. "Ally loves home-made preserves. It's all part of her nest-building mind-set right now. Domestic touches, you know. Thanks Jenni. I could never make this in a million years."

But then she spoke more seriously.

"At SCF, they are becoming more concerned on a daily basis about this Corona virus sweeping China. I know it seems a long way away, but with international air travel, now there's talk of one or two people with it in Canada and the USA and Italy. It seems to have a much higher mortality rate than normal flu."

"We should keep an eye on it, to see how it might affect our projects," said Isabel. "But with good management, it should be containable." And they left it like that.

When Jenni attended the RA Board meeting the following Thursday evening, she was nervous about the outcome of their discussion, because hard as Isabel might push to make the merger happen, the ultimate decision lay with the Trustees, whose watchword was always prudence and caution. They were a bunch of old people, with just a few notable exceptions, as Isabel had tried to co-opt fresh talent and some badly needed professional skills.

The constitution of RA still harked back to its original formation as a male dominated, evangelical organisation, and imposed few limits on trustee power. For example, there was no limit on the number of times a trustee could be reappointed for a further five-year term, so it pretty much remained the self-perpetuating oligarchy it was when Isabel had taken the helm.

Isabel had confided to Jenni that a major showdown was inevitable between her and the Board within the next twelve months. It would have happened earlier if she hadn't been on sabbatical for most of 2019, in order to write a book on climate change.

Every evening, Jenni and Jane spent at least half an hour online, talking together and sharing news and plans. It kept Jenni grounded, and helped her believe the events of the previous week hadn't been all in her mind. Jane was very positive about Jenni's ability to woo the Board over to setting up the Bristol link.

"You're far more confident than I am," Jenni said to her on Wednesday evening. "But I'll try my best. I just hope Isabel doesn't introduce me as a Catholic nun. To some of these elderly Protestant men, she might as well say I was a fanatical Islamist. Old prejudices die very slowly in the churches."

"You'll be fine," said Jane. "I know you. You can charm the birds out of the trees."

When it came to the Board meeting, held in a conference room they hired for the evening in their Office building, Isabel introduced Jenni, as 'Our West African Affairs Consultant', and gave her every encouragement. Jenni made her presentation, and relayed the enthusiasm of Pat and her colleagues in Bristol for the deal. There was a lot of discussion around the table, but fear of their charity going under entirely finally outweighed the natural reticence to take risks, of most of the old boys there. The proposal to seek a merger with GASP was passed by seven votes to four.

On Friday afternoon Jenni left the office as quickly as she could, claiming vaguely that she had an appointment. Luckily Isabel and the others were all in a meeting, and she was able to slip away without fuss.

She'd booked her train tickets online, and collected them at a machine on the Paddington station platform. It made her laugh, the very name, Paddington, but she was still in a state of nervous panic until the barriers opened and she was safely seated in her reserved window-seat on the way to Bristol. Perhaps she should find some wool and start a new knitting project if these weekend trips were to become the norm. It was clear that nothing formal was likely to happen by way of a merger before the end of February.

Jane was bouncing on her heels as she met her off the train in Bristol. It was past eight-thirty and the platform was filling with weary travellers heading home to their country cottages and weekend retreats away from London. Jane ran up to her and gave her a huge bear hug. She clung to Jenni with the warmest affection.

"Oh, I have missed you so!" Jane said. "Come on, let's get

home and go straight to bed."

Jenni couldn't resist a chuckle. "This is a rather different welcome from the first time we met. But I'm happy to see you still quite like me."

"Don't be horrible," said Jane. "Let's go."

She pulled Jenni by the hand through the station entrance and off towards the short-stay carpark.

On the way home, Jenni was able to explain the Board's decision in more detail than in the hurried late-night phone call the previous evening.

"They have agreed in principle, subject to all the checks and evaluation, and they also suggested we announce it at the AGM at the end of next month."

"So, you might be living with me full time by March? That will be fantastic."

"Are you sure you want me as a lodger? Isabel expects me to find a little flat somewhere. Can you really be doing with me all the time?"

Jane gave her a dirty look. "You didn't spill the beans to her about us, did you?"

"Spill the beans? That's another new phrase for me. No I didn't spill any beans."

"I knew you wouldn't."

"Of course not. But Isabel did say she understood how difficult it must have been for me, putting up with your bossiness, and sleeping in your little gym. Maybe I should go back in there tonight?"

"Oh, my God, woman, stop teasing. I have been dreaming of tonight every moment since you left last Friday."

Jenni had as well, although she chose to change the subject.

"Are you going to give me a golf lesson tomorrow, or a driving lesson?"

"You need a provisional license from the DVLA before you can start driving a car, and I also need to put you on my car insurance. But we might possibly make it up to the golf course this weekend, perhaps by Sunday afternoon. You claimed to have so much to learn about sex that I can't see us leaving the house much before then. Although I didn't see a lot of evidence of inadequacy last Thursday night."

Jane sounded as dominant as if she was out on the hockey field, coaching a young team, but when she glanced sideways at Jenni; her face betrayed a look of insecure excitement. Jenni realised the past week had been just as frustrating for Jane as for herself, and they were definitely in for an emotional and very physical weekend.

"Promises, promises…" she said, smiling. "Well here I am, ready to learn all manner of new things."

And she continued to talk in a similarly teasing way, all the way through the city, until they turned into the driveway of 27 Cropton Close, and stopped the RAV4 near the front door.

Chapter 24

More Than a Little Bit of What You Fancy

Coming back to Jane's place was a decidedly strange feeling. Jenni re-entered the narrow little house she had stayed in before, but, somehow, it now felt so different. The energy was totally transformed, and the previous cold, dreary and uncared-for atmosphere emanating from it, had quite lifted.

Jenni had never before thought very much about eastern ideas of Feng Shui and the power of energy fields within buildings, but there was definitely a new sense of very positive energy about Jane's home, which hadn't been there during her first visit. As she stepped across the threshold into the hall and then walked through into the sitting room, she could feel the transformation...so much so that she turned to Jane and asked, "What have you done? Why is it so different in here?"

Jane had slipped off her padded jacket and hung it up, and then stepped behind Jenni and did the same for her, pulling off the new red duvet coat she was wearing, and adding it to the coat-hooks by the door. The two jackets hung together, almost embracing each other, and Jenni then felt Jane's warm, strong arms enfold her from behind, with her chin resting lightly on her shoulder, and a wicked mouth quietly nip and then lick her ear lobe.

"Maybe it's because before last week, this was just a place where I slept at night and stored my possessions. Since you came, it's been a house full of hope and expectations. I am happy, so the house is happy."

"C'est trés woo-woo, for you."

"I love it when you talk pidgin French to me. You are so funny."

"Hmm...I aim to amuse. You are tickling me, Chérie."

"Turn around then."

Jenni turned and wrapped her own arms around Jane, and started to fulfill both her host's and the house's hopes and expectations, by doing some licking, and nibbling, and kissing of her own. They stood together, framed in the lamplight, and for five minutes, 'made out' as enthusiastically as any of Jane's fifteen-year-old pupils did behind the bike sheds. Jenni just couldn't get enough of the firm, slim strength and fitness which was Jane's body, and she simply adored being held close in the tight embrace which captured her whole body, and pressed it close to Jane's.

Jane suddenly seemed to realise the risks involved as she noticed the street-lamps outside, and said, "Whoops! Neighbourhood Watch alert! We should close the curtains, because we're in full view of anyone who looks in from the road. This is prime late-evening dog-walking time around here, and I'd prefer to keep our private life private."

She let Jenni go for a few seconds and went over to pull the curtains together across the bay windows.

"That's better. Now, where were we?"

"Thinking of going up to bed?" replied Jenni coolly. "I've eaten a snack already on the train, and I can't think of a single thing I need to do right now, other than to lie in your bed and make crazy love to you."

She spoke the absolute truth. She loved being fully out and open...to be here with Jane...to see her face light up with excitement and anticipation, and knowing they would end up in bed very shortly.

It was such a new feeling, just as the happy vibes in this house were so new and stimulating. It was almost like a new birth, being promised generous helpings of physical and mental pleasure, which were now hers for the taking. She just couldn't believe her luck, or blessing or whatever it might be called, to have found this joy.

"Let's go," she murmured quietly, with her best French growl, and held out her hand for Jane to lead her upstairs.

When they reached the bedroom directly above, Jane again drew the upstairs curtains and blocked out the dark winter night, and also the suburban streetlights and clustered houses, surrounding their haven. Then she walked back towards the bed, lifted the duvet and felt the bottom sheet beneath it.

"Just before I left home to fetch you, I turned on the electric blanket," she explained. I want you to be as warm as toast, so you won't need pyjamas. Come and feel the sheet and see if you think it's OK."

As Jane switched off the blanket, Jenni went across and put her hand down on the bottom sheet of the bed. "Wow. That is *incroyable*. I never felt anything like this before."

"Are you telling me you've never slept in a bed with an electric blanket?"

Jenni gave Jane a look which conveyed what she thought of that stupid question.

"In tropical Africa? Or in an austere convent back in the early nineties? Give me a break."

"Then, my dear, you have so, so much to learn about the miracles of modern technology. I've turned it off now, but I think you'll find it a very liberating experience."

"I can't wait, but can I just check my phone, to see if there are any messages from Sophie or the RA people? I did leave the office in rather a hurry this evening."

Jenni began to pull her phone out of her pocket, and start to fiddle with it, but Jane took it from her, and switched it off.

"Nope, Niet, Non," she said. "Let's go off the grid, just for this weekend. You are mine, all mine, so let's set ourselves free from the pesky phones for now."

Jenni had a momentary twitch, worrying that she was neglecting her duty to her girls in Brussels, and to her work colleagues at RA, but Jane was right. They should live in the moment, not be addicted to checking messages and voice mail all the time. She smiled, and didn't ask for her phone back.

Jane obviously didn't want to waste any more time. She pulled her down onto the bed and began, very efficiently, to undress her lover.

She was soon tugging off Jenni's boots, her socks and then unzipping her trousers, new black ones which were part of the large gift-package of clothes she'd bestowed on her the previous week.

"I'm glad to see you've ditched the old torn jeans."

Jenni shook her head. "Oh no, not ditched, just put safely away for another day. Anyway I think you secretly quite liked them, didn't you, even if you wouldn't admit it?"

"I liked what was under them, your legs and very neat and tight-looking little arse, as I like looking at them now."

Jane had now undressed Jenni down to her underwear below the waist, and was already pulling her out of her layered tops.

"Keep the bra on, for now! We can have fun with that later," she said.

"You like playing dollies with me, don't you."

"Yes."

"So, why can't I enjoy the same game? Strip off for me as well, Jane Walkley. Let me see the goods on offer tonight, eh?"

Jenni lay back on the pillows, her arms folded above her head. Her eyes flashed just the right degree of confidence and command to Jane, who was surprised and aroused to see this new, dominant side to her lover. Here in her bed was a new woman, not an emotionally exhausted and conflicted nun, but a free and assertive partner, who was, after all, eight years her senior, and used to controlling the lives of a thousand girls. She hoped she hadn't underestimated her too much, or appeared condescending without realising it.

Jane looked at Jenni straight in the eye as she obeyed her. She could feel Jenni's molten gaze on her as she took in her well-toned arms and shoulders emerging from her fleece top and tee shirts. Then she undid the button of her Rohan trekkers, unzipped them and let them fall to the floor. She removed each piece of her clothing methodically and neatly and hung them over the chair. Finally she was out of the trappings of civilisation, with her cross-trainers and her socks also removed and placed under the chair. She stood a foot or so from the bed, now wearing only her sports bra and skimpy black pants.

"Stop now?"

"No, keep going, darling."

Jenni's low alto voice, and its gentle but firm instruction, made Jane's crotch tighten with desire. It was so wonderful to feel this pure lust, after so many barren years. For Jenni this must seem like emerging from a trek across the thousand miles of the Sahara desert! If they needed any more things in common than they already had, then their pent-up frustration and past-histories were well matched.

Jane stepped out of her pants, and then pulled her bra over her head. No-one had ever looked at her with that white-hot heat coming from Jenni. It was unequivocal, single-minded, and predatory. Jane swallowed.

"Now come here," Jenni whispered, and Jane came to her, joining her in the bed, and covering her with her body. She knew that within a few minutes Jenni would be penetrating her, making love to her with her hands, rubbing, and stroking and stimulating her clit into a frenzy. But what she hadn't anticipated was the dexterity of Jenni's mouth, especially her tongue and her teeth as well.

Naively, she supposed, she had assumed Jenni really would need lessons in all the various sexual techniques lesbians might use to make love and bring each other to orgasm. But this clearly wasn't the case! Perhaps this woman had been teasing her before. Whatever the case, there was no doubt Jenni was very much in charge now, very much calling the shots, as she prepared to give Jane the time of her life.

Athletic and fit as she was, Jane could hardly keep up with the pace at which Jenni moved. Her body started to float out of her control, as Jenni spread her legs as wide as was comfortable and then pushed herself down the bed so she could concentrate her attention on the magic triangle at the top of her legs, the little banks and inclines and the opening to her innermost core, her essence.

Jenni began by kissing her belly, then her hips, and then her inner thigh. She was working her way up and inwards, and when she finally dropped a kiss on the edge of her vulva, Jane's body responded automatically and instinctively. It lifted up of its own accord throbbing insanely against the relentless mouth, which teased and licked around her clit and then went further, deeper into her inner core. The kisses turned into something much stronger, devouring her, sucking and drinking...It was almost unbearable. She had to come, she couldn't resist...

"Harder, deeper, please..."

Jenni seemed to know exactly what she was doing, or maybe, she was simply naturally gifted. She brought Jane to an orgasm, which shuddered through her entire body, and left her almost weeping with relief and happiness. Then, in a few short minutes, she did it again. And again.

There was seemingly no messing with this woman, this quiet, apparently introverted soul with the husky voice and the grey eyes fringed with long lashes, who walked as quietly as a cat. In bed she transformed into a tigress. She'd impatiently thrown off her own underwear already, to get better naked access to every sensation. They made love for hours, and by the end of the night Jane was so sated, she didn't know what to do with herself. Her muscles ached and her bones felt like liquid.

She lay there, with Jenni's curly hair tickling her breast as she slept the slumber of someone who had definitely earned their rest. She didn't want to disturb her, so she stayed as still as she could, but she was simply too excited, too ridiculously happy, to be able to sleep.

How could this have happened? How could a couple of weeks make such a change to a person's life? From bleak despair to exultant joy. Oh, pray God, she didn't do anything to mess it up! She couldn't bear to think of any future which didn't have Jenni Argent in it. Then she realised wryly, that she was bringing a God who she still didn't believe in, into the picture yet again. It was beginning to be an unfortunate habit.

Jane did finally nod off between five and six in the morning. She was astonished to find, when she struggled awake and opened one eye to look at the radio-clock by the bed, to see it was already 11.50. This was unheard of! For the first time in her life, she had slept right through most of Saturday morning.

The pretty woman whose body she was supporting, who was wrapped over and around her, even now was still asleep. They were melded together, breast to breast, hip to hip, and pressed even closer, for Jenni had a leg thrown over Jane's thigh and tucked firmly up against her crotch. Jane moved herself against it, indulging in the soft, sensual pressure which nursed her vulva, rather than enflaming it further.

Jenni felt the movement, and while still half asleep reached down and captured both Jane's hands. She lifted them above her head, and then kissed the uplifted breasts, which rose so enticingly under her face.

"You have beautiful breasts," she murmured, sensing that Jane was awake. "They are so evenly matched, so full and curved, without being heavy or floppy. They are perfect. I could lie here and kiss them all day." And she was as good as her word, nuzzling the left nipple and then teasingly playing with it in her mouth.

Jane smiled, "So, you're a breast girl, are you?" But then as her nipples started to swell and tingle again, she protested, "Oh, how do you do this? Are we going to start all over again? I am not sure I can cope with any more going and coming, right now."

Jenni was rather busy but still found the means to speak, and openly scoffed at her.

"Where's your stamina? I thought you were the current Ladies Golf Champion for North Avon, or was that a little lie? I would have expected more upper body strength than this."

"It's not *upper* body strength we're talking about here!" Jane decided Jenni had had it all her own way now, for far too many hours. "Come on, stop molesting my breasts and let me take my turn."

She managed quite easily to toss Jenni over onto her back, and pin her down beneath her. Having achieved this, she began to do to Jenni, pretty much what had been done to her for so long the night before.

As their love-making reheated close to boiling point, she could feel Jenni's passages open up to her mouth, begin to expand and contract to the rhythm she set. Her tongue found the elusive G spot and had great fun licking and torturing her lover, who was moaning and bouncing on the bed within minutes.

The clock downstairs started to strike noon, just as Jenni climaxed with such force that she nearly threw Jane off the bed, and gave what could only be described as an orgasmic scream.

This was great, thought Jane, with a smile like a Cheshire cat. That would teach her lover a lesson or two, but she regretted slightly that she lived in a terraced house. The sound-proofing in these new-builds wasn't the greatest, even if her neighbour through the adjoining wall was thankfully in her eighties and pretty deaf.

The weekend had quite a few sessions to go however, and Jane had further tricks up her metaphorical sleeve! She pondered how much Jenni might warm to the idea of toys? Perhaps they, like electric blankets, would be a new and novel experience for her? The very idea aroused Jane once more, and she pressed herself yet again up against her lover.

Jane had some sex toys in the drawer under the bed, sad reminders of a hot and dirty weekend away she had once spent with Felicity, but now unused for years. Their batteries would be completely flat by now. She wondered as she lay there, if she needed to go out to buy some new ones. Oh, the dilemmas of having a hot new lover in one's bed!

Chapter 25

Par For the Course

It was past three o'clock in the afternoon before the pair of them finally stopped making love and heaved themselves out of bed. Jenni followed Jane into the shower and then looked at herself in the bedroom mirror as she began to search in her pack for some respectable clothes to wear.

She had never spent a day like this, nearly eighteen hours continually devoted to the sybaritic pleasures of the flesh, and when she looked at her reflection, she saw the face of someone drugged on pleasure and the delights of physicality... drunk on lust.

Her eyes looked slightly unfocused and her pupils were enormous, almost as though she was high on narcotics. Her hair stood on end like a wild woman's, and her body was pink and flushed still, very different from her normal rather sallow skin-tone.

Crazy, crazy day! She was also aching in places she had never felt any muscle strain before, like someone does who goes horse-riding for the first time. But all in all, Jenni felt wonderfully, stupidly, wickedly, happy. It was as though thirty years had been stripped off her age and tossed aside, like all those decades of self-discipline and deprivation in search of spiritual perfection.

There was no going back now. She'd crossed a spiritual and sexual Rubicon, and had come into her own mind and body. She was also rather hungry, and very thirsty, though, and once dressed, padded downstairs in her socks, to find something to eat and drink.

Jane, who looked like she'd been rolling in the hay for several hours, grinned broadly as she saw her enter the kitchen.

"Here, I've made us some coffee. But I suggest we might go out for breakfast or afternoon tea, as we could call it now. There's a good restaurant and café up at the Golf Club. I can show you around and introduce you to some of my friends who will probably be there. It's only a few miles from here. Would you like to do that?"

"I'd love to, if you would. Yes, let's do it."

So after a couple of cups of freshly brewed coffee, they set off again in the RAV4. Jenni decided she should pay more attention to how a car actually worked, as her ambition to learn to drive as soon as possible hadn't gone away. She watched Jane slide the gear into reverse and then back out of her driveway and set off.

"This car is automatic, I take it?"

"Yep. But if you want to learn properly you should do it on a car with manual transmission. I might fix you up with a professional driving instructor. Passing the driving test in the UK is far more technical these days than just learning to drive. The lessons are very structured to cover all the bases, and you have to pass a written theory test before you get close to the practical exam. But I will still add you to my insurance and you can practise all you like. Just don't crash us and drive us into a ditch, because I don't have duel controls, like a driving instructor would. I suppose we can make the time, especially if we don't spend as much time in bed as we have this weekend."

"Shame!" laughed Jenni and then smiled broadly as she interrupted Jane making exactly the same comment.

"We can do just what we want, my love," said Jane. "We are consenting adults, and it will be nobody's business but our own. We need never go out at all, if you prefer. That would be fine by me."

"Yes, I'm sure it would be. And I'd like it as well. But you are also my friend as well as my lover, and I want to be able to meet your friends, and share your interests. There's so much I've yet to learn about you."

"Oh, I doubt it. I'm not a complicated person. Very boring really."

Jenni shook her head. "I disagree. I think that's a mask you wear for self-protection and to hide behind. You are one of the most fascinating people I have ever met. Like a rose, tightly wrapped. I know there is more to you than you let on. Just as there is to me. But the unique thing about you is that you are what you said you were the other day. You are wonderfully sound, and honest. You're maybe a games player when it comes to sports, but you don't play psychological games with people. So many people do that. They end up hurting others and hurting themselves. I've learned the hard way that we can only be ourselves. Like someone said, all the other roles are taken."

"You are very philosophical," replied Jane quietly. "But I trust you too, even though you talk a load of tosh at times."

Jane turned off one of the roads leading out of the city centre and was climbing a hill to the east. Then she swung in to the right, down a tree-lined drive and came across the low buildings of a purposely-built club-house. Jenni was amused to see she parked in a designated space marked "Ladies' Captain." It all looked very formal and organised, and exclusive, obviously not for the *hoi-poloi*.

A well-kept series of long greens forming the golf course spread away from them in three directions, with a putting green beside the main entrance, and then a low roof of a sizeable driving range stretched out to one side. On the first floor, with floor to ceiling plate glass windows, she could see a restaurant overlooking the greens, and it was up to this room that Jane led Jenni, having signed them both in at the reception desk below.

Jenni could now add "Tea in a Golf Club" to the growing list of her new experiences. The wintry day outside was still chilly, but the sky was bright and there were several sets of players in little groups of twos and fours making their way up and down the fairways. It was fun to watch them through the windows, while sitting snugly inside, at one of the several round tables close to the view.

Jane passed her a menu. "What would you like? The food here is all good."

After a few minutes, a waitress came over and greeted them.

"Hi Jane, how lovely to see you. Have you been playing today?"

"No, not today. Maybe tomorrow. But I'm here with a friend. Let me introduce you to her. Jenni, this is Kim, who works here on weekends. Kim used to be one of my students, and is now studying at Bath University. Kim, this is my very good friend, Jenni Argent."

Jenni offered her hand in the French manner, to the bright young thing in a pony- tail who wore a striped apron over a black polo-shirt and trousers.

"How do you do, Kim?"

Kim shyly took her hand and shook it. "I am well. Welcome to the Club, Ms Argent. I hope we see you again."

"Oh, you will," promised Jane. "You will."

"Are you ready to order?"

"Yes, please."

Jenni decided to order a full English cream tea. 'When in Rome, do as the Romans…' She'd missed breakfast, and lunch, but wasn't yet quite ready for dinner. She wasn't entirely sure what to expect to see arrive, but it sounded interesting.

"Make that two then," said Jane, and when Kim had disappeared to make up the order, Jenni said, "So what's a scone?"

Jane looked at her very sternly. "Now, look here. I still think you've a lot to learn, Madame Principal. One day I hope I can put you up for British citizenship, but you're obviously far from ready to take the test."

"Let's get our priorities right, shall we," replied Jenni, blandly. "In the list of things to learn, I'd say the priorities would be, '1. Advanced lesbian sex. 2. How to drive on the wrong side of the road. 3. The rules of Golf. 4. Becoming a respectable English lady.'

"Which of those can I leave to you to teach me, and which would I need extra coaching for? Numbers Two and Four, probably, am I right?"

"You're so sharp; I wonder you don't cut yourself." Jane pulled a face.

"I know. I'm hilarious, aren't I?" laughed Jenni. "But look, here comes our order. So now you can explain it all to me. Tell me please, what is the difference between High, and Low Tea and what if I want a Medium tea? Why do the English put cucumber in their sandwiches? And why do you put milk in my tea-cup before the tea?"

Jane was right. The food at the Golf Club was excellent and they both ate their way through an enormous array, including jam and cream scones, egg and cress sandwiches, as well as all the other goodies on offer.

Jane was very happy to see her loved one tuck in, and also to note how her face was definitely less gaunt and angular than it had been the week before. Jenni would probably never be fat, but a lifetime of living on rice, vegetable and beans with scant amounts of protein and even less fat, had left her at least fifteen pounds lighter than the ideal for her height, and Jane was delighted to see her looking a little rounder in the face.

Her wariness about dairy products seemed thankfully to have ended as well. Seeing her negotiate her way around a large cream meringue was a joy to behold, and Jane had to sit on her hands to prevent her openly kissing the cream off the end of her nose.

But they were out in public, and in an arena where Jane was well-known, so she behaved with suitable decorum. Before the light faded, after they finished the food and emptied the tea-pots, she pointed out to Jenni the groups of players straggling down towards the eighteenth hole, and began to explain the basics of the game of golf to her. They could see the people by the flag on the last green clearly through the window.

Jane plucked at Jenni's sleeve and said, "See that guy playing to finish the game on the 18th hole? He's obviously tired and cross, and losing his concentration. Look at his putting. Whoops, there he goes again, missing the hole by an inch."

"I've counted him take three shots now," said Jenni, "No…four, and five! Now he's flinging down his club, and conceding the match. Poor man."

"Many a game is won or lost on the putting green," said Jane. "But see the little club he's using, we call it a Putter."

"Pronounced like Butter, not footer?"

"There you are, we'll have you talking golf like a pro in no time!"

Jenni looked hard at the man and his friends, and said quietly, "I don't just want to talk Golf. I want to play it," and she sounded very determined.

As the last players left the green, and came into the Club House, maybe for a quick round of drinks, Jenni said, "So, you say there are eighteen holes, and you have to play them all to make up a round of golf? That seems a very long walk."

"Yes, up to five miles on a decent championship course. On some smaller municipal courses, you might find nine holes which you play twice. And the different holes are different lengths. We call them a Par 3, or a Par 4, or for a very long hole, you might even get to Par 5."

"What does that mean?"

"It means that the 'Par' for the course, referring to the number of shots you need to get from the tee to the hole by the flag. It's the agreed standard, indicating a competent golfer should be able to go from the start, the tee, to the hole, in three, four or five shots. The first shot, or the drive, is the longest, where a good golfer will hit a ball straight up the fairway for 200, 300 or even 400 yards. Then the second shot might be a shorter one, a pitch which takes it onto the green, and ideally just one or two putts will take it to the hole."

"So the putt is to put it in. That's easy enough to understand."

"Yes, but it's not putt as in foot or put. It's putt as in butt."

"Hmm, maybe I'm not as good at talking about golf as I thought. When can I have a go?"

"I'll book us into the driving range tomorrow. How about 12 noon? Can we get up for them? An hour should be enough to start with. You will be given a bucket of balls, and I'll show you how to swing and hopefully hit a few of them. Then you'll be tired after an hour on the range, and so we can eat lunch here. They do a great roast beef Sunday lunch."

"But when can we do the long walking around the course thing?"

"If you want to, we can have a round tomorrow after lunch. You could be my caddie and I'll explain the different clubs as we go."

"Different clubs? But I thought you only belonged to this

one?"

"Not clubs. Clubs. The thing you hit the ball with. And we can take your balls, the ones you kindly bought me last week. When you start to learn golf, you'll be bound to lose quite a few in the rough."

"'In the rough?' That's another new expression for me."

"That's when you hit the ball by mistake into the long grass, and you've no idea where it's leading you off to."

This seemed to spark something inside Jenni and she said,

"Jane, I think you and I have been leading each other off 'into the rough', ever since we met."

"You may be right. But is that so bad?"

"I don't think so. It's exciting, and so little was exciting in my life recently. Who knows where we will come out? I find the idea of being in the rough very appealing."

"It's the opposite from the straight and narrow."

"Yes, isn't that a lovely thought? I am so very tired of the straight and narrow."

And they both started to laugh.

Into the Rough

Chapter 26

Naturally Gifted

Taking Jenni to bed for the third night revealed even more joys and delights for Jane. She had pulled into a garage on the way home to fill up the car, and slyly picked up a packet of AA batteries while she was paying for the fuel. Then as they cuddled together in a freshly made bed, complete with the warmth coming up from the electric blanket, she pulled out her little collection of toys and gadgets, and explained to Jenni what they were for.

Jenni was suitably intrigued and impressed how technology had developed so interestingly while she had been busy teaching European languages to her young students in West Africa. As Jane passed them over to her, one by one, she looked at them all, fascinated by the variety of shapes and sizes.

The use of some was obvious, and flagrantly vulgar.

"I'm not sure I want a large purple plastic dick inside me." She threw it away with a good cricketer's over-arm toss across the room. "Your mouth and hands will do just fine. But what's this, this little thing with rabbit's ears?"

"Oh, that's a classic. Do you want a demonstration?"

Jane switched it on. Their laughter and later screams carried on into the night. Finally, Jane produced a shiny smooth little tool, rather like a lozenge. It had a remote control switch, which, when she turned it on, made the gadget begin to vibrate and throb of its own accord.

"What's that?"

"It's a cute control game or an instrument of torture if you prefer. You wear it inside you. We go out to dinner, and then when I choose to, I can push the on switch up, and enjoy watching you squirm and try not to come while you are talking to the others around the table. Good fun, eh?"

"It would be, if I had my hands on the control, not you. I'd like to see you wear it at one of your Golf Club dinners."

"Yeah. The Past-Presidents' Annual Formal dinner. That would be just great," Jane said ironically, but Jenni was just warming up.

"We should have a bet on something. Then if I win, that could be my prize!"

Jane could see Jenni was getting far too keen on the idea, and decided to divert her attention to things much closer to home.

"Oh, no, I'm putting all these away now. They are only for party nights and special occasions. Let's put the lights out and just make non-technological love."

Jenni snuggled happily against her.

"Yes, let's. I love you, Jane Walkley, do you know that?"

"I'm getting there. I just need reassurance. Show me again, won't you?"

And they kissed again in the darkness, as she shut down the lamp.

Mid-day on Sunday saw them back up at the Golf-club. It was a bright, clear frosty day with the car-park nearly full. Jane was glad she'd booked a bay in the driving range for Jenni's first lesson.

There was another student part-timer in there, who handed them a wire bucket of balls, and asked if they wanted to borrow some irons. He obviously was new; otherwise he'd have known that Jane, who was second only to the Club Pro in her ranking at the Club, would obviously have her own bag of clubs. Jenni seemed bemused by the whole set-up.

"So how does this work, exactly?" she asked as Jane handed her the wire bucket and led the way down the line to the one spare bay. She carried just a couple of golf-clubs, drawn from her own bag, a seven and a five iron.

"Well, in order to get the ball to go where you want it to, you need to develop the muscles and flexibility in your neck, shoulders and hips. To begin with, it won't feel natural. You'll move what you should keep still, and you will keep still what you should move. Also, your grip on the shaft of the club will feel weird to start with, but eventually it will become an extension of your arms. So to start with, we are not even going to touch the balls. We are going to practise a few gentle swings."

She took Jenni's jacket from her shoulders, and hung it up behind. Then she pushed her into the bay. Jenni's first lesson began.

"There, see that little peg in the ground. That's your tee. It's like a cup on which you sit the ball. That's why we call starting to play a hole, teeing off. Now stand back from it, with your feet about two and a half feet apart, and take the golf club. This is what we call an iron. The bigger, longer clubs are called woods. They are for driving the ball longer distances. Now hold the shaft just down from the top, and link your fingers together. Your right-hand's little finger fits into the crook of the first finger on your left hand, to steady them both."

Jenni did as she was told, and gripped the iron.

"No need to cling on for dear life. Just gently but firmly. Now swing it back and forth, but keep your eye on the tee. When a ball's sitting there, you want to keep your eye firmly on it. Back and forth like a clock pendulum. You don't need to go higher than waist height right now. Good. That's good."

"Can I try with a ball?"

Jenni was obviously keen to get on with it, so Jane lifted a ball out of the bucket, and placed it on the plastic tee.

"Look down the driving range. There are markers at fifty, a hundred, two hundred and three hundred yards, then four hundred, as far as you can see."

"Do we have to get all our balls back?"

"Goodness, no. We'd be killed if we tried. The balls fly all over the place. At the end of the day, one of the staff will go around with a mechanical ball catcher and retrieve them all for the next day."

"So, what would be a good shot?"

Jane laughed, "For your first attempt, hitting the ball at all. Most people miss it and take what we call an 'air-shot.' If you keep your eye on the ball and let the club hit it square on, you might pitch it twenty yards. Follow the ball with your eye. You're aiming for a nice gentle arc in the air, not flat. So go on, have a go."

"Don't laugh."

"Of course not."

"Right. OK, then."

Jenni stepped back and inch or two, wriggled her wrists, looked down at the ball, and swung back the seven iron. It hit the ball dead on, and the little white object flew up in the air like a bird, and went on, and on, and on.

"Holy moly!" Jane followed its course down the range until it landed neatly on the grass in front of them a good hundred yards away.

"How did I do?"

"How did you do? Don't play games with me, woman. You're no novice. You've played golf countless times, haven't you?"

"No!"

Jane looked completely sceptical.

"No, I promise!" protested Jenni. "It's the first time I picked up one of these things. It was just a fluke. Beginner's luck probably. Can I try again?"

"Sure. I'll shut up this time. See if you can do it again, like that."

Jenni replaced the ball with a new one, and set up the tee once more. Then she swung back, and without seeming even to know what she was doing, sent that ball flying even higher in the air, and even further down the range, as straight as an arrow.

"Hey, I like this. This is fun." She pulled out a third ball.

Jane didn't know what to say. She'd been playing golf since she was seven, when her father had first taught her the basics on the municipal course in Chester, but she had taken years to master that effortless swing and central twist in the hips that Jenni was demonstrating.

If her friend was being truthful, and she had no real reason to doubt her, then Jenni was an absolute natural. This could alter everything. If Jenni was consistent with all her shots, and played a good short game, then they could go out and enjoy a round together, and she wouldn't have to make constant allowances or spend half the time looking for Jane's balls in the long grass.

"You keep practising like that," she said, after six balls had spun away without any of them being anything other than perfect shots. "I'm going back to the car to fetch my woods. I'd like to see how you deal with those."

Jenni had worked her way down half the bucket by the time she returned, and there were still no casualty balls anywhere near their bay. Jane handed over her favourite wood, a big driver with a face nearly as wide as a tea-plate.

"Here, love, swop over to this."

"Wow, it's lovely, but the shaft is much longer."

"Yes, you need to stand much further back from the tee, with your legs wider apart. It will take practice, but now you can swing it much higher behind you. Still think of your hands driving the club back behind you, as if you were drawing around a clock-face. The torque in your body will provide the spring action, so when you come back down on it, you can hit the ball with sufficient force to make it fly up into the air and go racing off towards the flag."

Jenni took up the position, gripped the shaft of the club once more, looked down at the ball, and whoosh, pushed her arms back and then forwards with such speed, Jane could scarcely see the ball go. Then she looked up in the sky and saw the tiny projectile shooting above her. It flew against the blue, and then came down in a perfect arc, exactly three hundred yards away.

"That wasn't as good as I'd hoped," said Jenni, annoyingly.

"Wasn't it?" Jane tried hard not to sound sarcastic. "Why not try again?"

"OK, and honey, I can see now why you love golf so much. It's such fun, isn't it? I'm going to try and hit the back fence, see if I can do this properly."

Jane didn't like to tell her the back fence with its high nets was a good four hundred yards in distance away, and only the best and strongest golfers ever made it, especially in a straight line.

Jenni though, in the single-minded, understated way she

had just addressed the ball, pulled back and used the driver to such good effect that the ball went up and right out of sight, flying west into the wintry sun. They waited, bemused, and then they could just make it out, coming down beyond the four hundred yard marker. It was a shot which the best golfers in the country would have taken pride in.

"Not too bad?" asked Jenni, "for a beginner?"

"No, not too shabby at all." Jane took the driver from her, and just for fun, put a ball on the tee for herself. "Are you sure you weren't Canada's under eighteen champion, back in 1987? I can't believe you're not kidding me here."

"I promise, and I'm just knocking balls about by instinct here. You'll have so much to teach me, darling."

"You're just being kind. I think you're a golfing natural, and we'll have to get you a handicap ranking as soon as possible."

"A handicap? What's that?"

"I'll tell you over lunch. For now, I just want to see if I can come anywhere near your ball. I haven't played on the range for ages, so I could easily mess up here."

Jane took the shot, and was pleased that she didn't disgrace herself at least. It landed fifty yards nearer to them than Jenni's balls, and she'd sliced it a little, but out on the course it would have done its duty. Seven, maybe eight, out of ten.

"Wow, you look wonderful. You play very stylishly."

"Thank you darling. Let's finish the last few balls, and then go over to the restaurant for lunch. I booked us a table by the windows again. All I can hope is that you're lousy at putting. Otherwise I'll be handing back the women's champion cup next summer, without any contest."

Jenni took back the driver and finished off the bucket of balls. Jane adored watching her, and was pleased she could honestly claim she was a teacher first, and a competitive player second. Otherwise, Jenni's natural talent at a game she had never played before would be driving her crazy.

"Come on, I want to show you a traditional British Sunday lunch," she said as they returned the empty wire basket and went up the stairs into the Club House restaurant. "The Yorkshire Puddings here are to die for."

"What are Yorkshire Puddings?" asked Jenni, and Jane was relieved she still had some things to learn after all.

The rest of the afternoon was even more of a revelation to Jane. After lunch, which Jenni did take a gratifying interest in, she followed Jane out on to the real golf course like an excited child.

"So, what did you say I could be? Your caddie? Does that mean I have to carry all these clubs around the whole way? That will be character and muscle building."

"No, darling. I have a motorised trolley. So they'll drive themselves."

Jenni's eyebrows shot up under her tousled curls.

"You mean, your golf clubs can drive themselves, but I can't?"

"It's a figure of speech. We'll give them a steer now and then, but there's a little electric motor in the trolley, so we don't have to do much pulling."

"Wow. You know that English expression people use, when they say, that they're gob-smacked..."

"Yes."

"Well, I never knew where I would use it before now, but I can honestly say, my gob is smacked. Just think what African women could achieve if they had an electric trolley to carry their farming tools, or their water, instead of having to carry everything on their heads!"

Jane gave her an affectionate push.

"Yes, I see your point. But let's get going. We are not supposed to share clubs out on the course, but I am the team captain and this is your first round, so we can both use my set for this afternoon."

"You mean I get to have a real go?"

"Of course. I've picked you up your own score card, and a pair of golfing gloves from the pro's shop-now, let's get started. I also have a spare pair of golf-shoes in the car. They are compulsory on the greens."

Out on the course, Jenni had an attack of nerves at the first hole, and her opening drive wasn't the blistering 400 yarder it had been on the range. But it was just as straight and as balanced, and Jane kept pace with her, so they didn't get too far apart. Jenni seemed incapable of hitting a poor shot, which wasn't so good from a teaching point of view, as Jane had no need to show her how to chip in from the rough, or how to hit her ball out of a bunker.

She tried to tell herself that she was simply playing as Jenni's partner, to support her, but the game was still stretching her, and she was watching the scores with alarm. She had intended giving Jenni the beginner's handicap of 36, but the woman was taking most of the holes very close to or even on par. Even on the greens her balls seemed hypnotised and rolled politely into the holes as if they were magnetically drawn there.

They made it all the way around the entire course to the 18th hole, before the daylight began to fade, with Jane finishing only three shots ahead. When Jenni said to her, "Oh, thanks for letting me play. I can see why you are the champion of the women's section of the club," it was all Jane could do not to tear up both their cards. Still, she adored this woman, and could be proud she'd found a secret, undiscovered genius in the fifty year old, and hopefully soon to be ex, nun.

Even Jenni, though, readily admitted she was tired by the end of the afternoon. Jane's second best golf shoes were rubbing her heels slightly, so when they reached home she was very happy to sit on the sofa and put her feet up on Jane's lap and let her nurse them.

They were enjoying a welcome mug of tea sitting in this position, when Jane's phone went. Jenni watched as her lover answered.

"It's probably my mother," Jane mouthed as she picked it up, "She normally calls this time on a Sunday."

But it wasn't her mother, it was Isabel. She sounded very agitated.

"Jane, I know this is a very long shot, and a bit of a daft question, but do you by any chance know where Jenni might be? We've been looking for her all weekend, and I need to speak to her very urgently. She's not picked up her messages since Friday evening."

"Er, well," Jane looked across to Jenni, with a somewhat

guilty look on her face.

"I think we're busted," she whispered. "It's Isabel and she wants to talk to you." And she switched the phone to loudspeaker so she could eavesdrop on the conversation and then handed it across.

Into the Rough

Chapter 27

Busted

"Hello, Isabel."
Jenni could hear the astonishment come down the phone.
Isabel almost shrieked in surprise.

"What? Are you telling me you actually there in Bristol,
staying with Jane? What on earth have the two of you been up
to? I would have thought you'd have seen enough of each other
last week to last a lifetime."

Jenni took a deep breath and prepared herself for the
confessional. But it was clear Isabel hadn't yet guessed. She
must have taken at face value both hers and Jane's bland
summaries of their week together.

Jenni felt guilty for deceiving her new friend and boss, but
was secretly rather pleased they had pulled it off even as long as
they had. She must have developed a far better poker face than
she'd realised.

"Er, no, we're fine. Jane has been teaching me to play
golf."

"And is that all? Why has your phone been off all weekend,
and why didn't you pick up your messages?"

"Well, I'm so sorry. I turned my phone off. We've just
been a bit busy. Now, is anything the matter? Why did you need
to speak to me?"

"I am phoning on behalf of your friend Sophie in Brussels.
She found out on Friday that they are bringing the trial of the
people traffickers forward to this coming week, and has been
trying to reach you ever since. The girls are naturally terrified,
and they need you to go to Brussels at once. She doesn't think
they will have the courage to give evidence unless you are there
with them. Can you call her immediately and hear all the details

from her?"

"Oh, my God, yes of course! I'll do it now."

"And Jenni, darling…"

"Yes?"

"Pass the phone back to Jane, will you, please?"

Jane was shaking her head madly; guilt all across her face, but Jenni thrust the phone into her hand, and then jumped up and ran upstairs to get her own IPhone.

She left the two old mates to sort out their own issues, but she suspected Isabel would scoop out the real story of their relationship and about the weekend before very long. That woman had a mind like a gimlet, and was actually far tougher than Jane.

In the bedroom she was relieved to see her IPhone was still almost fully charged, having been switched off for two days, and she called Sophie at once.

It was just as Isabel had relayed. Sophie said the sudden notice of the trial and the summons to the Courts had come as a huge surprise, and the girls were totally unprepared. All the trauma of their abduction and kidnapping had returned, and she was having great problems in reassuring them they had little to fear.

Jenni thought quickly, and said, "Don't worry. I'll be there with you all as soon as possible, with luck by the end of tomorrow morning. When does the trial begin?"

"*Jeudi,* - Thursday. But the lawyers will want to start prepping them tomorrow. They are the key witnesses, apart from Marie-Krystina and you, and without the girls, they say the case may not be so easy to prove."

"I'll be there. I'll get the Eurostar train. It will be quicker than flying. Can you put Leontine and Patience on the phone, please?"

Jenni switched to Swahili and began to console and comfort her young charges. She was on *Facetime* with them for over half an hour.

Downstairs, Jane faced the music with Isabel.

"Golf lessons, eh? Pull the other one. Jenni has no interest in golf…or has she undergone a personality transplant since you two met?"

"Bel, you are wrong. The woman is in fact a golfing genius. She completed her first round in eighty-two. Can you believe that? And she swears she's never lifted a golf club before! You should see her play! So yes, I have been giving her lessons, not that she hardly needs them."

"I bet golf isn't the only thing you've been teaching her, is it? I can read you like a book darling. I can tell by the sound of your voice that something else has happened. Are you going to tell me all about it, or carry on this little charade of not warming to her?"

Jane gave in. She was, after all, dying to tell someone about Jenni, and Isabel was the obvious choice as a confidante. If Jane insisted, she knew Bel would keep it to herself and not spread the word all around the office.

"We are still getting to know each other, and I didn't want to say anything straight off. Things are difficult for Jenni, you must see that. She has to make some big decisions about quitting her order, and we need to keep it confidential until that's settled."

Isabel was audibly excited now. "What are you saying, that you haven't just made friends, but you connected with her on a deeper level? Have you actually kissed her?"

Jane wondered how to gently bring Isabel into the real world.

"Er, yes."

"More than once?"

"Bel, she is wonderful, everything I could ever want in a lov…"

"You haven't been to bed with her?!"

Now who was the puritan?

"Isabel, get real. We've hardly been *out* of bed since Friday evening, except to go to the golf course. Jenni is the hottest woman I have ever met. She's sex on legs."

Silence.

"Have I shocked you? You did say you needed to hear the truth"

"But she's a celibate nun, darling. Have you been taking

hallucinogenic drugs?"

"No I haven't, not even one, and Jenni may have been celibate for the last three decades, but trust me, she isn't any longer."

"Jane, you are a minx. So, did you seduce her?"

"No, I tried quite hard to be good. Actually it was she who kissed me first. She blew my mind away."

"Blimey. If this is real, and I'm not down a rabbit-hole here, tell her I need her side of the story as soon as she feels up to telling it."

"O.K. But don't tell anyone else, will you? I suppose you can confide in Bryony, because I know you won't be able to keep it a secret from her. But we are going to need our privacy. There are so many things to work through."

"I understand. Jane, you can trust me on this one. But I also understand now why Jenni was so positive about moving to Bristol for the GRASP job! Silly me, I thought it was all down to her passion for African girls' education!"

"She's still keen on that, but she's also showing something of a passion for me, boring, dreary, plain old me."

Isabel was clearly having none of it. She said, "Sister Jenni is a woman of excellent taste. If she agrees with me that you're the bee's knees, then you undoubtedly are. I couldn't be happier for both of you, my love. Let's talk again tomorrow. And tell Jenni if she needs to go back to Brussels it won't be a problem. She can stay there as long as she wants or needs to."

Jane came off the phone and went upstairs in search of Jenni. The implications of this call for help from Sophie was slowly dawning on her.

She had no idea how long legal proceedings might take place in Belgium, but she imagined they would probably be long-winded. If Jenni stayed away for weeks and weeks, then she would miss her miserably.

Somehow the English Channel seemed a big barrier, and she would be stuck in school for at least another three weeks until the half-term holiday in late February. And wasn't the Corona virus spreading across Europe? She needed to talk through the situation and do it at once.

"Jenni, darling, where are you? Talk to me…"

Jenni was sitting in the bedroom chair, trying to book an online ticket for the Eurostar train to Belgium for Monday morning. Jane sat at her feet and hugged her around the knees.

"Do you have to leave tonight? Please say you don't. I understand how important it is you go to Brussels, but stay one more night, please!"

Jenni looked down at her beloved and nodded her head. "Yes, I am staying with you tonight, my love, just as planned. I did have a crazy idea I should go back to Trixie's tonight, but I can go straight from Paddington to St. Pancras station for the Eurostar. You see how expert I'm becoming about London transport!"

"I'll take you to the early train. But how long will you be away in Belgium?"

"I have no idea at this point. My priority is to care for the girls. Sophie has done a splendid job, but she is almost into her seventies, and I can't neglect them all any longer. If I could take you with me…"

"I know," Jane interrupted. "If I could, I'd come with you like a shot. But I can't leave school until the half-term break. If you are still in Belgium then, can I come over for the week?"

"Of course, and I'll call you every evening. We'll work it out, honey."

Jenni fondled Jane's spiky blonde hair, and then ran her finger lightly down her cheek, with real affection in her eyes. It turned Jane's heart to jelly.

She said, "Let's go to bed now. I know it's early, but I want every minute with you I can get."

"Just let me book my seat on the Eurostar, and then I'm all yours."

"What a lovely thing to say. While you do that, I am going to phone my mother. Then we can safely trust there will be no more phone calls this evening."

"Will your mother suspect something, do you think, like Isabel has?"

Jane pulled a face. "No, I very much doubt it. Mum is so convinced I am on the shelf for life, she will have to meet you in person before she'll even begin to be convinced otherwise.

She'll think I've invented you just to keep her off my case."

"Then that's one trip we have to make," said Jenni firmly. "As soon as Brussels is sorted, you can take me to Chester to meet your mother. Then we can make it official."

"Are you really sure? Will you give up all your old life, and commit to me, truly?"

"Truly. I love you Jane, with all my heart. I want to be with you forever."

"Me too. It's actually very romantic, isn't it? Love at first sight, just like Isabel predicted."

"Isabel tends to be right about most things. We owe her a lot. Now go and shower or do whatever you need to do to prepare for tomorrow, and I will buy my Eurostar ticket. I'll meet you in bed in thirty minutes."

"I'll turn on the electric blanket." Jane jumped to her feet and went to set things ready for another long, sweet night of loving.

Chapter 28

In the Grey Light of Dawn

Their last night together, for who knew how long, was sweet and sensual, and full of everything one might imagine about consensual sex between two adult women. It was also restful. After a long day out on the golf course, an evening of physical activity in bed led to them both falling asleep before midnight.

Neither woke till six am, when Jane's alarm made them both leap out of bed and scurry about getting ready to leave the house. They grabbed a cup of tea each, and then Jane drove like the clappers and left Jenni at the station with five minutes to spare, just in time to jump onto the London train. They just had time for a quick, fevered kiss, and a hug.

Jenni was so relieved she had her passport with her, so she could transfer straight over to the Eurostar express leaving St. Pancras at 9.30, and true to her word, she was in Brussels, catching the tram to Sophie's place and in her apartment by the early afternoon, Brussels time.

The girls came home early from school, smart and tidy in their uniforms. They looked so young, and so scared, that her heart went out to them, and she sat down on Sophie's long couch, with her arm around each of them, to hold them and give them courage.

Then, at 5pm, the chief detective from the original investigation came around. She brought with her, Marie Krystina, the Director of *Sisters in Solidarity*, whom Jenni had met back in early January. *SIS* was a Brussels based agency devoted to the fight against sex trafficking and the rescue of its victims.

The four women all gently rehearsed with the two

teenagers the questions they might be asked and how they might reply. One obvious issue would be their understanding of the lawyers' questions, and their ability to answer clearly in a language which wasn't their mother-tongue.

"I can translate for either or both of you, if you need me to. But we must give the court warning of that and they may ask for a court appointed translator," said Jenni.

The girls looked alarmed, and asked why it would be necessary. "To ensure objectivity, and also so I don't put words in your mouth. I will probably be called as a material witness, myself."

"The time-frame is very short," commented Sophie. "Why have they brought the case forward by so much?"

The woman detective said, "There are rumblings about the Chinese virus beginning to spread, and if it gets bad, then they want to clear the prisoners on remand out as far as possible. In many ways it's lucky for us. Some cases normally take five or six months to come to court."

Once the interview had finished, the girls went back to their room to recover and relax by playing a video game on their laptops.

The detective asked Jenni what her plans for them were. They had another appointment the next day, to run through the case again, but this time it would be in the office of the prosecuting counsel, down in the city centre.

"I'm not sure. I need to ask them what they would like to happen first of all, before we start making big changes to their lives. My gut reaction is that in the future they will both be far happier back in Africa. But they come from quite different countries and cultures."

"They are both settling happily in school here, and Patience has picked up French very quickly. I would be so sorry to lose them," said Sophie. "If they qualify for asylum, they will both have a home here with me. They already feel like my own granddaughters, and they are devoted to each other. It may break their hearts to split them up." She was obviously unhappy to think of her young charges being taken from her.

"Bless you," said Jenni, "I know how much love you have for them. We certainly won't do anything hasty."

After the girls had gone to bed, Sophie had Jenni all to herself, and she asked, "And what about you, Cherie? Something has happened to you in the UK, hasn't it? You seem different somehow, less conflicted about your calling. And your clothes have certainly smartened up!"

Jenni chuckled. "Yes, I have smartened up, but only because someone very sensible has kitted me out with a whole new set of clothes. She…"

"She? So is this a new friend, someone who has given you this new, happy expression on your face?"

Jenni looked out of the window at the darkening skyline. Sophie's apartment was high up on the fifth floor, and the lights of Brussels were twinkling away below them. She considered her words carefully, and then decided to be candid with Sophie, whom she had known since she was a young teacher, and also a very unhappy and discontented nun.

"Yes, it's true. I've fallen in love. I never thought I could be so happy. It has been a complete revelation."

"So, who is the lucky woman? I presume it is a woman?"

"Yes. She…she is Isabel's best friend. Isabel introduced us. She's called Jane, and she teaches sports and physical education. She hated me at first, even before she met me. Because I was a nun, and she is an atheist."

"But now?"

"Now, none of that matters. She is actually much less strung up about God than I am. She has helped me begin to heal from my terrible relationship with the Church."

"You are going to formally resign your Orders then? Turn this trial separation into a divorce?"

"Yes. There are many things I am unsure about, but this is quite certain for me. I have to leave. But it is like a divorce, and it may be a messy one. I know I will walk away with nothing, not even a pension. It sounds very materialistic, but I have to think seriously now about how I can manage without the convent's support. It's their money which keeps Leontine and Patience here and provides for them. It is also their money which funds my job in London and will enable me to relocate to Bristol to be with Jane."

"God will show you the way. Maybe you should pray for a solution."

Jenni snorted, though with a wistful undertone to her scorn.

"All my prayers have been marked 'Return to Sender' for a long time now. I think God has deserted me years ago, even as far back as Rwanda, when we had all the massacres."

"My dear friend. You are the expert on matters theological. I am a mere lay-woman, but sometimes the most banal proverbs speak the most clearly. God certainly does work in mysterious ways. How can we know the future? Even this year of 2020, who knows what lies just around the corner?"

"Who knows indeed? I often think we are like tiny ants on a patch of grass, discussing the politics of China, if we try to understand our own existence, let alone debate the mind of God."

Jenni looked at Sophie's clock ticking away on the mantelpiece. "If you excuse me, I need to make a phone call." Jenni went into the corner of the sitting room where Sophie had made her up a bed, and phoned Jane, on the dot of eleven o'clock, (ten o'clock in Bristol), just as she'd promised she would.

Jane jumped like a startled hare when the phone rang, interrupting the chimes of Big Ben on the ten o'clock news. She'd been waiting for the call with her phone in her hand for the last fifteen minutes. She'd been so frightened Jenni wouldn't call, that she nearly sobbed with relief when she heard her voice.

"Hi, how are you? Did the journey go well? Tell me everything please. The house is so quiet now, and like me is simply waiting for you to return."

Jenni brought Jane up to speed with everything that had happened, and the sound of her beautiful husky French-Canadian accent slowly brought Jane's anxiety level down and did wonders for her blood pressure.

"What about you? How was school today? Tell me about your day," said Jenni, and Jane, with a certain amount of prompting, started to share the events of Monday. It was always a difficult day, with a full programme of seven forty-five minute lessons, and a home-room session in addition.

Jane was in charge of a form of stroppy fifteen-year-olds, because she was considered one of the minority of teachers who could keep excellent discipline with that age-group, and she began to tell Jenni, about the challenges. One boy in her form had been arrested over the weekend for being in possession of quite a stash of cannabis, and the police had called at the school to interview some of his friends. So that was her lunch break effectively wiped out. A pretty normal day in a secondary school, but it still felt good to share it all with Jenni.

When they finally decided to call it a night and each retire to bed, Jenni said, "I told Sophie about us this evening."

"And how was that?"

"It felt the right thing to do. She was completely in agreement. She understood when I said I am resigning my orders, whatever the outcome financially."

"We'll be fine. I told you not to worry. I can look after you. You'd be surprised how much I earn, after nearly twenty years at the coalface. We will manage to get by without problems, my love."

So as Jenni rolled herself up in Sophie's sleeping bag and went to sleep, she wondered if the prayers she hadn't dared to make, were going to be answered by her lover after all, by the woman who didn't believe in God. Life could indeed be an experience of heaven or hell, but whatever it was, it was certainly a mystery!

Into the Rough

Chapter 29

Going to Court

Jenni was right. The Belgian courts did insist on their own translators to help the girls give their testimony. This took some time to arrange...not for the languages in DRC which had after all been a Belgian colony not so long ago, but for Patience's language from Northern Nigeria. Jenni couldn't have helped with that anyway, so she didn't argue.

Her main role was to act *in loco parentis* for the girls, support them in all the police and legal interviews and also sit with them in court as they were forced to see again the men who had trafficked and kidnapped them. On the first day, when the charge sheets were read, Jenni realised that her girls' ordeals had been just a part of a much longer list of appalling crimes which had come to light. That didn't include the earlier murder of Isabel's fiancée Carrie, which would be a separate case altogether.

Multiple men, and a few women, were part of the conspiracy and trafficking racket, but most had already pleaded guilty, and thus didn't have to appear as defendants in this trial. However the men who had been at the heart of Leontine and Patience's ordeal refused to accept the charges, and were now in full view with their defence team, appointed by the Court on their behalf.

They had badly underestimated their victims, assuming they would be too afraid to stand up in open court and accuse them, but once they were in the courtroom, both girls seemed to gain a confidence beyond their years. Jenni and Sophie, who had come to the hearing as well, were very proud of them. Leontine and Patience each spoke clearly and looked straight into the eyes of the men who still inhabited their nightmares.

The defence lawyers had little to fight them with, even though they tried. To begin with, they merely quibbled about Patience's memories of her initial trafficking and kidnap, challenged her horrific version of events and tried to say there had been a case of mistaken identity. But Patience was fearless. Unlike Leontine she had been raped more than once during her several months of travail, and she was able to identify a scar on her attacker's lower belly. As the prosecutor pointed out, she wouldn't have been able to see it if he hadn't dropped his trousers to force himself on her.

The defence lawyer then tried to claim the sex had been consensual, but Patience's eyes had flashed with anger, and she had said loud and clear," I was fourteen years old, and a virgin. I was crying for my mother all the time he was raping me." This alone was enough to move some in the jury box to dab at their eyes.

Leontine's story was different, but no less powerful. It made a compelling testimony. She had been tricked into leaving the safety of her boarding school by being told she had a sick aunt who needed her to go to care for her. But instead, she'd been beaten and pushed onto a flight from Kinshasa to Brussels.

She told how Stephanie had met her in the queue at the airport and was someone she thought she could trust. Then when she saw her walk up the plane to the toilet, she managed to pass her a phone number, which Stephanie used to contact her former head teacher and foster mother, Sister Jenni Argent, in Canada. She had only been held for ten days or so, before she was rescued, but during that time, she had fought so hard against being raped that she'd been badly beaten up. Once in Belgium they had been locked away without adequate toilet facilities, chained to a radiator and half starved.

Then Jenni was called to the stand. She told the court of Leontine's life as her pupil in DRC, how her behaviour had been exemplary, and that she was top of her class. She told how she'd been contacted by Stephanie and Alana in London, and how together, with help from the police, they had found and rescued both girls. She stressed how co-operative the police had been in the matter.

For the Court, Jenni had dressed as formally as she could.

She'd even gone shopping to buy a black shirt, black skirt and black shoes for the occasion, and wore her crucifix around her neck, something she normally kept in a little case with her missal. As she looked across the courtroom at the scumbag, Sonny Alvares, the man who had abducted her little Leontine, she had nothing but hatred and disdain for him.

"Why had you gone back to Canada?" demanded the defence attorney. "Wasn't it your own abandonment of your duties which led to your pupil being exposed to vice?"

"I was ordered to leave Africa on medical grounds," she replied calmly. And here Jenni gave the correct medical term for her parasitic form of recurrent malaria.

"Leontine was in the excellent care of my successor as the school principal, who is an esteemed local citizen of the DRC, and also supervised by the matron in charge of the girls' boarding house. They cannot in any way be blamed for her abduction and exploitation."

Here Jenni crossed her fingers as she spoke, because she did believe her successor had been far too lax in the supervision of the girls' dormitories, and especially blamed her for not sending immediate word to her in Canada of Leontine's disappearance. But she didn't want to divert the focus from the men in the dock.

Jenni could appear very commanding when she wanted to. Her posture was upright and regal, and her voice was low and authoritative. She made a very good witness for the prosecution, and the largely Catholic members of the jury immediately warmed to her and believed every word she said.

The other really positive thing to happen was that Steph Hunter, Jenni's colleague now at RA, was also called as a witness to tell the jury how she had encountered Leontine on the plane from Kinshasa. Jenni was delighted to see her, and they embraced warmly when they met at the courthouse

Steph said nothing about hearing anything from Isabel about Jenni's relationship with Jane, so she had obviously been true to her word and kept it confidential. But Steph and Jenni were already becoming close friends, and Jenni wanted to tell her and Alana personally, as soon as things settled.

"Are you staying overnight here in Brussels?" she asked Steph as they sat together in the waiting room for witnesses.

"No, just for the day. So much work to do at home. The attorneys said I could probably get away with this one time in court. But I can come back again if it drags on."

Then Steph was called to the stand and was offered a translator. She accepted, saying she could speak and understand basic French, but was not completely fluent in it.

She told the story Jenni already knew well, how a frightened little girl had met her in the queue at Kinshasa airport, and on the plane had followed her to the toilet and pressed a scrap of paper into her hand with a phone number on it...Jenni's number as it turned out.

She then saw her being intimidated by a man sitting next to her in the economy section of the aircraft. Could Stephanie identify the man? Yes, he was one of the defendants, Sonny Alvares.

At that point the Court broke for lunch. Sophie, Jenni and Steph scooped up the girls and took them to a safe and quiet restaurant for lunch and told them both how well they'd done. Now the trial had begun, both Leontine and Patience seemed to have grown in confidence and empowerment. They certainly ate a good lunch, and when all the party returned to court for the second half of the sitting, they were optimistic of a positive outcome.

By the end of the day, details of the near-miss in the police raid on the first suspected location, and then the subsequent rescue from the migrant doss house near Antwerp all came out. Jenni could see the girls were now flagging. They didn't need to relive the horrors they had gone through in that house, and she and Sophie took them home. Marie-Krystyna was now on the witness stand, and she could easily convince the jury of the defendants' guilt.

When the day's proceedings finished, Marie-Krystyna phoned Jenni and Sophie and told them what they'd missed in the final hour or so.

"It all went crazy. The two defendants started to fall out in public, and then came to blows. The police had to tear them apart and take them down to the cells in hand-cuffs. I don't think it did their case any good, and their defence lawyers were throwing their files down on the desk in disgust."

"Any idea how long the case will go on for?"

"Oh, it might be over by the end of tomorrow. It depends how long the jury takes, but I don't think they will want to spend a weekend in a hotel. And I don't think they'll call the girls again. People could see how traumatic it was for them. Unless you hear otherwise, I think they could go back to school tomorrow and certainly by Monday."

Jenni told Jane all of this and much more, during their usual late evening phone-call.

"So, you might be able to come back this weekend?" Jane's voice sounded so hopeful and happy, Jenni was very tempted.

But she said, "No, not this weekend. I need to see this out, until the final verdict is given, and then I need to sit down with Sophie and decide what happens to the two girls. But I'll be with you as soon as I can, trust me. I love you, sweetie."

"So, it's sweetie now? Not honey anymore?"

"My honey, my sweetie, my baby, my lover, ma chérie. You are all of those things, and more."

"OK, cool it. Any more of this and I won't be able to sleep. I'll be pulling out the toys from the drawer under the bed and making use of them by myself."

"Don't you dare! You wait for me. I'll sort you out when I get home."

"Home to me?"

"Naturally. Where else?"

And hearing that, Jane whispered something so raunchy into Jenni's ear, that she made her revert to her nun-like persona, and whistle through her teeth with shock at the suggestion.

"Ha, I thought that would shake you up a bit! Goodnight, darling," laughed Jane.

"Goodnight." And Jenni went to bed, almost wishing she herself had one of Jane's toys to play with. The woman certainly knew how to keep her sexuality on high alert, even across the many miles from Bristol to Brussels.

Into the Rough

Chapter 30

Truth Will Out

Marie Krystyna was right. The Jury retired to consider their verdict at noon on Friday, and by four, they emerged from the jury room with a unanimous verdict. Both defendants in the trial were pronounced guilty on all charges and were taken away until the following week when the Judge would pronounce their sentences. Prison was inevitable, but whether for ten years, fifteen or longer, she had yet to decide.

Jenni had sat in the public gallery of the court for the morning and went back to hear the verdict. That evening, with the girls, Marie-Krystyna and Sophie, she allowed herself a little indulgence as a celebration that the nightmare was over. She bought a large chocolate gateau on her way back to the apartment, and they all shared it. She took several photos of the little party and sent them across to Jane, and to Isabel and Stephanie, so they all could join in the good news.

On Saturday, she and Sophie took Leontine and Patience to the movies, to watch a new film. It was fun enough to distract the teenagers from their recurrent traumas, and a treat for girls from Africa who had never sat in front of a big screen. In fact, Jenni had to admit she hadn't been to a film in a movie theatre for nearly forty years either, and was surprised how much she enjoyed it, even passing the large paper cups of popcorn back and forth, and watching twenty minutes of adverts and trailers before the movie started. It was dubbed from English into French, but Patience seemed to follow the plot without problems. The stunts were scary, and the characters seemed to leap out of the screen at them.

On Sunday, she sat down with Sophie and the girls and asked them what they wanted to do next, stay in Belgium, or return to Africa?

"We want to stay together, like sisters," was the first thing Leontine said. Then she added, "I don't think Patience would like the Congo."

"Can we stay here with Tante Sophie?" asked Patience. "We love her, and we are settling into school OK. We've made some friends, and the teachers are cool. They don't beat you, ever, not like in my old school."

Sophie said, "As you can imagine, I have been doing lots of research about the girls' situation. There are very strong grounds for them to be admitted into the EU as unaccompanied asylum seekers, or they can simply apply for student visas to study here. That would be straightforward as long as we can show they can be financially self-sufficient and not dependent on state aid."

"Could we do that, Mama Jenni?" The girls pleaded with her, their eyes full of positive hope and relief. "Then we can stay to take our baccalaureate examinations, and even go to college here."

Jenni couldn't refuse them the hope, but neither could she promise them something which she didn't know if she could fund.

"We'll do our best. I will try my hardest to sort everything out. But don't worry about anything right now. You both have six months' visas, which will take you through to June, so you are quite secure here until the end of this academic year, if Tante Sophie doesn't mind."

"Mind? These youngsters are the light of my life," protested Sophie. "Now, let's have the rest of that cake!"

Later, after the girls had gone to bed, she said to Jenni, "Cherie, don't let your concerns for the girls' futures change your decision about resigning your vows. You deserve to be as happy as anyone else in this world, and your whole life so far has been one of self-sacrifice, and putting the needs of others first. I have a little nest-egg, and I can also draw down my pension, so even if I give up work. I can support them myself."

Jenni squeezed her hand. "That's lovely, and Jane also has said much the same. But they are both my responsibility and Leontine especially is my child. I sat with her mother on her death-bed and promised her I would always care for her. I know you will love and nurture her, but I need to ensure she and Patience can have enough money to stay in Europe legally and decently. I'll see to it, don't worry. I am going to write a letter tomorrow, to the Archbishop's Council and to my Mother Superior in Quebec, and we'll see what transpires."

Jenni woke early the next morning and sat at Sophie's kitchen table to write a long and reasoned letter on her lap-top. It was perhaps one of the most important and sober letters of her life, but she told the truth, laid out all the facts, and didn't prevaricate about her sexuality and her wish to form a life-long partnership with another woman. She asked if there was any fund available to support the two girls, whose story the sisters in the Convent already had been made aware of. She didn't ask for money for herself, but for Leontine and Patience.

Then before her courage failed her, she printed off two copies on Sophie's printer, begged her for a couple of envelopes, signed and inserted the letters. The addresses she knew by heart, from sending her monthly reports on the progress of the Mission School for all those many years. She wondered what to put as the return address, but after a moment's thought, typed out clearly, *27 Cropton Close, Bristol.*

This was too important a communication for email. She needed it to be in writing. Finally, as she went across the city to the courthouse, to hear the judge impose the sentences on the traffickers, Jenni stopped into the central Post Office, stamped and pushed her letters into the box for overseas mail. It was done.

Justice was also done. It took another five days of waiting, but then Sonny Alvares went down for a minimum of fifteen years for kidnap and trafficking, and his fellow defendant was given two sentences, one for multiple cases of trafficking, and one for rape, to be served consecutively. He wouldn't be getting out of jail for at least twenty years. There was a ripple of applause across the courtroom, and the Judge had to order everyone to pipe down or be expelled from the proceedings.

Finally, it was all over. The week of waiting for sentencing had enabled Jenni to pour extra support to the girls, and help them with their studies. She would always be there at the end of the phone, or on Facebook to chat, but formal guardianship was now in the hands of Sophie.

Jenni realised how much tension she'd been carrying in her neck, even though she had hoped for a good verdict, and felt a heavy load drop from her shoulders as she went out of the courtroom. Her first call was to Sophie, then she texted Isabel, and Stephanie, and then she wondered if she might catch Jane in the mid-morning break-time and rang her phone as well.

"Guess what, honey? I'll be back with you tonight. It's all over. The nightmare has ended for us. I know Isabel's is still to come, but at least she can know the monster that killed Carrie is already in jail for these new crimes. He won't be hurting any other women for a long, long time."

Jane was bouncing up and down at the other end of the phone. "Thank God. Call me when you get to London, and tell me which train you'll be on. I can't wait. It's seemed like an eternity since I saw you. Oh, and please take care. They say the Covid19 virus is spreading across Northern Italy. It could easily get to Belgium!"

"I will. Don't worry. I love you. 'Bye."

Chapter 31

Chester is a fine City

"So this is the famous Jenni? It is good to meet you at last."
Muriel Walkley held out her hand and welcomed her
daughter's new 'friend' into the hallway of the old family home
in Christleton, the prettiest and most affluent of all the villages
close to the city of Chester. She had a house on the outskirts of
the village, near to the canal, but she could still hear the church
bells, walk to the shops, and watch the children run past her
gate to the primary school.

It was now February half term, two weeks after Jenni's
return from Brussels, and Jane had brought her beloved north to
introduce her to her mother. Jenni, whose own mother had died
when she was too young to remember her clearly, wasn't used
to such a relationship, and to begin with she felt slightly shy.

But she quickly fell into a cordiality with Muriel, which she
could tell would grow into an easy relationship. Years living
with older nuns had made her sensitive to their ways, the need
to speak up clearly, and not take offense at criticism kindly
meant.

Jane chipped in, "Now you know Jenni is not just a friend,
Mum. Jenni is my lover. And I've asked her to marry me."

"My dear," Muriel led Jenni into the lounge while holding
her hand. "Jane always did like to call a spade a shovel. But if
this is the case, I'm really happy for you. Dare I ask you what
your reply was?"

Jenni looked at her prospective mother-in-law. She could
see some of Jane's forthright honesty and straightforwardness in
her eyes, and she had the same shock of hair sticking up above
her forehead, although in her case it was pure white. She was
obviously in her late seventies, and shrinking somewhat because

of osteoporosis, but her voice was firm, and she seemed brisk and cheerful.

"I said 'Yes'." She dipped her head close to Muriel's ear. "It was such a pretty ring, I couldn't resist."

She winked and held out her left hand to show a clean cut but shiny band of sparkling stones. The night she had returned from Belgium, Jane had met her at the station, took her out to Bertarelli's and fed her lasagna before producing that entrancing little black box.

Jenni continued, "We did have a little fight about who was going to propose to whom, but Jane won, as you might expect. I want to give her a ring in return, but she says her hands aren't made for jewellery, so we are still battling on that one."

They sat down to lunch, and Jane was chatting to her mother about a variety of things. She described how school had gone that term, how Jenni had a natural talent when it came to golf, and that she was teaching her to drive. Jane also said she wondered if they had time to meet up with her two brothers and their families while they were in Cheshire.

Muriel had bought most of the lunch from Marks and Spencers, but it was very good, and they were tucking into apple crumble and M&S custard, when she suddenly said what she was thinking. She turned to Jenni and confided to her, "I'm so happy to see Jane finally settled with someone who will be such a good match for her. She's certainly had some funny crushes before."

Then she said to Jane, "Darling, whatever happened to that strange nun you said came to stay with you? You know the one who forced you to make marmalade? I was worried for days afterwards that you might do something crazy like fall for her! I'm so pleased to see you're now with a sensible person like Jenni instead."

The fiancées stared at her and then caught each other's eye.

"Should I?" asked Jane silently, by raising her eyebrows. But Jenni shook her head gently, meaning, "No, let it go. We can have fun telling her our story later." But they were both close to laughter.

Jenni decided to talk to Muriel more openly about how much she loved Jane, and how she hoped she could always make her happy. Muriel, in return was equally open about how she had accepted Jane's sexuality and never questioned it.

"I had an aunt who was the same way. We took it for granted. She lived with a woman called John, who had an Eton Crop, which was a very short hair-cut popular before the Second World War. They had four dogs, and raised chickens and ducks. Stayed together sixty years, and died within a month of each other, well into their nineties."

"What do you do for a living, Jenni?" Muriel then asked, as though she was remembering she should show some concern for her only daughter's future financial prospects.

"I used to be a teacher, but I've just been asked to run a charity based in Bristol, to do with girls' education. I'm moving down from London after this week, to take up the reins."

"And will you be living with Jane in that terrible little house?"

"It's not terrible at all. I love it, and Jane says we can re-decorate, and re-carpet it"

"I always thought she'd do better in a nice country cottage. There are some lovely villages to the north of Bristol you should explore. But that's up to you of course. Now while you're here, Jane must give you a tour of Chester. It's a fine city. We have some excellent Roman remains and very attractive architecture."

Jane decided a walk around the centre of Chester would be a good idea. Jenni was entranced, like any respectable North American might be, by the medieval double-storey rows of shops, the old city walls and the Roman amphitheatre. Then they went down towards the River Dee and took tea in a classically olde-worlde tea-shop on Bridge Street.

"Try the tea-cakes. They are extravagantly good here."

"We seem to spend all our time either in bed, or stuffing our faces in tea-shops. I am putting on far too much weight."

"No, you're not. It's good to see you no longer looking like death warmed up, a skinny bag of bones. I like something I can hold on to."

So Jenni ordered a pot of tea and a toasted tea cake. It was yet another item of British cooking she'd yet to experience.

"What did you make of my Mum?" asked Jane.

"She's lovely," said Jenni, "but I'm terrified she will share your views on nuns and cast me out when she finds out the truth."

"You'll convert her in a twinkling of an eye," smiled Jane, "Just as you converted me. I was a blind, prejudiced fool, and I'd be grateful if we could conveniently forget how badly I initially treated you. Anyway, I now love all nuns, especially after you had your decommissioning letter back from the folk in Canada. They were so gracious."

The tea and tea-cakes arrived and Jenni saw how delicious they looked, with the butter oozing out and dripping down the sides. The days of stretching rice and cassava leaf stew around twenty or thirty hungry mouths were now far behind her, but she was still grateful for every time her stomach felt full.

"Yes. I had absolutely no idea that the dowry my father had paid when I'd entered the Convent back in 1988 would be returned to me, with thirty- two years of compound interest added to it. $200,000, can you believe it? Now that was a miracle. And isn't it great they have also set up an educational trust fund for the girls, so they can stay on in Belgium?"

"It really is," agreed Jane. "You know, with your little nest-egg and my savings, and what we'd get from the house, we can afford to move to the country, like Mother suggested, if you want to, darling Jenni. How would you like to live in a cottage in the Cotswolds, with roses around the door?"

"Sounds divine, as long as there is a golf-course within walking distance. You know I'm getting rather addicted to the game, just like you."

"We won't be able to play golf for much longer, if this Covid19 virus spreads any more. I have a nasty feeling it is not going to go away. According to Isabel, Steph and Alana are thinking of bringing their wedding forward in case there's a ban on big gatherings by the end of March."

"Let's wait and see, shall we? One day at a time. I've learned to trust in God again, not the one I have hated and feared for so long, but an altogether better spirit. Now I've left the convent, I think we've stopped quarrelling. She is coming closer, an elusive divine spirit of love. She gave you to me, after all."

Jane reached over and cupped Jenni's face. "If it is love we're talking about, how could I not believe in it as well? Now eat up the rest of that tea-cake or I will steal it off your plate. Then I want to take you shopping. There's a discount sports shop in the retail park near Chester, where we can buy you a complete set of new golf-clubs. Call it an early birthday present."

"You sure do spoil me," sighed Jenni.

"By the way, when is your birthday?"

"Not till September."

"Close enough. And we must get you a trolley as well."

"With a funny little motor?"

"Absolutely."

Jenni put the last of the teacake into her mouth. The girls in Brussels were happy and now financially secure. She'd left her Order with its full blessing and understanding. And she had the love of her life sitting opposite her. Life couldn't get any better.

There was just the faint cloud of anxiety about this ever-growing threat of the Corona virus creeping over their horizon. But with Jane beside her, nothing could surely really go wrong.

They left the café together, and strolled down to the river, and then next to the Bridge across the Dee, Jane gathered Jenni into her arms, and kissed the taste of butter off her face.

"I love you, Sister Jenni; even if that's the last time I ever call you that."

"And I love you too. Now explain to me all about all the different golf clubs. Why do people have so many? It's very confusing. And what's the difference between a sand wedge and a sandwich, and what's a Big Bertha….?"

Jane sighed, and pulled her sleeve to make her keep up, as they walked away. "We'd better get back to the car and drive over to the sports outlet. I can see I've got my work cut out here…"

Jenni laughed, and let her lead the way.

About the Author

This is Maggie McIntyre's fifth novel. She has written fiction for most of her life, and especially enjoys writing about women in love with women. She believes a good story can inspire, entertain and also console in times of trouble. It also has the power to break down barriers of hatred and fear between people, and help people live their lives to the full. Her home is in the north of England, but she travels extensively, when COVID allows.

Learn more about Maggie by following her on her Facebook
page, Maggie McIntyre Author and her website.
www.maggiemcintyreauthor.com.
email: maggie@maggiemcintyreauthor.com

Other titles by Maggie McIntyre you might enjoy

Isabel's Healing by Maggie McIntyre
A devastating car accident leaves Bel broken, but when a young assistant steps into her life, could Bel learn to live again?
Available from Amazon KDP (ISBN 9798650898733)

Heatwave by Maggie McIntyre
Can'fresh out of school' Catriona Sinclair win over media mogul, Katherine Konrad, or will she get a little too close for comfort to the legend's notorious past?
Available from Amazon KDP (ISBN 9798677313929)

Wildfire by Maggie McIntyre
Sequel to Heatwave. An outing to meet Cat's family turns into a weekend fraught with danger. Will the challenges they face strengthen their love in the face of a natural disaster or will it prove too much to handle?
Available from Amazon KDP (ISBN 9798550424988)

A Girl on the Plane by Maggie McIntyre
Sequel to Isabel's Healing. Beautiful but reckless Stephanie Miller and her lover Alana Byrne set out on a Christmas road trip, which will determine their future, and also save lives.
Available from Amazon KDP. (ISBN 9798573921822)

Other Great Books by Independent Authors

Nights of Lily Ann: Redemption of Carly by L L Shelton
Lily Ann makes women's desires come true as a lesbian escort, but can she help Carly, who is in search of a normal life after becoming blind.
Available from Amazon (ISBN 9798652694906)

The Woman and The Storm by Kitty McIntosh
Being the only witch in a small Scottish town is not easy.
Available from Amazon (ISBN 9798654945983)

Sliding Doors by Karen Klyne
Sometimes your best life is someone else's.
Available from Amazon (ISBN 9781916444386)

Stealing a Thief's Heart by C L Cattano
Two women, a great escape, and a quest for a soulmate.
Available from Amazon (ASIN B085DW2MZ7)

Maddie Meets Kara: Remember Me by D R Coghlan
Who is her enemy? Who is her friend? And what really happened that night?
Available from Amazon (ASIN B085WP5CDF)

1140 Rue Royale by Karen D. Badger
A gripping story of love and redemption in the most haunted mansion in New Orleans. (2017 GCLS Award Winner - Paranormal)
Available from Amazon and Badger Bliss Books (ISBN 9781945761003)

Yesterday Once More by Karen D. Badger
Will Jordan risk her own future to save the life of her lover who died before she was born? (2009 GCLS Award Winner – Speculative Fiction)
Available from Amazon and Badger Bliss Books (ISBN 9781945761027)

Other Great Books by Independent Authors

<u>Over The Crescent Moon</u> by Karen D. Badger
Spencer Bennet wakes up alone and injured on a deserted beach in Hawaii, only to find her world turned upside down. (2019 LesFic Bard Award Winner in 2 categories – Action/Adventure & Historical)
Available from Amazon and Badger Bliss Books (ISBN 9781945761263)

<u>A Shadow in Love</u> by Karen D. Badger
Mackenzie Caldwell loves to hike the trails of Sedona, Arizona. Zangendar Tafadon has traveled from a distant galaxy to escape a dying world. Life will change forever for Kenzie and Zan when their paths literally cross on the hiking trails of Sedona, Arizona!
Available from Amazon and Badger Bliss Books (ISBN 9781945761324)

Printed in Great Britain
by Amazon

80538229R00129